DOGNAPPED

TWISTED KEY
publishing

2022

First Printing: 2022

ISBN 978-1-63911-036-0

Twisted Key Publishing, LLC
www.twistedkeypublishing.com

Ordering Information:
Special discounts are available on quantity purchases by corporations, associations, educators, and others. For details, contact the publisher at the above listed address.

U.S. trade bookstores and wholesalers: Please contact Twisted Key Publishing, LLC by email twistedkeypublishing@gmail.com.

CONTENTS

1
MR. BINXLEY IS MISSING

"Mr. Binxley's been kidnapped!" screamed a high-pitched voice on the other end of the police dispatcher's phone. "He's g-gone." The voice went from screaming to sobbing.

"Sir? …Sir?" repeated the dispatcher, worriedly.

"Yes…?" came a raspy response.

"What's your name, sir?" asked the dispatcher gently.

"Milton. Milton Hardy, the third."

"And you said that Mr. Binxley has been kidnapped?"

"Yes," he sniffled.

"From your residence?" inquired the dispatcher.

"Yes, someone broke in and kidnapped him. He was resting in his travel crate…."

"Wait, Mr. Hardy, did you say he was resting in his travel crate?"

"Yes, I went out for my morning coffee and—"

"Mr. Hardy, is Mr. Binxley your pet?"

"You say that as if it's a bad thing. Mr. Binxley just happens to be a Cavalier King Charles Spaniel," said Mr. Hardy, aggravation filling his voice. "He also just happens to be worth over a quarter-million dollars."

"Geez!" whispered the dispatcher under his breath.

"Mr. Hardy, I show your residence as 1217 Vine Street. Is this correct?"

"Yes, 1217 Vine Street," he sniffled once again.

"Okay, Mr. Hardy, I've dispatched Detective Taylor and Officer Holland—they're on their way."

2
DOGNAPPED

Detective Taylor ran his calloused hand through his graying hair. He sniffed loudly and scratched his large bulbous nose. It seemed that over the years, the larger his nose grew, the itchier it got. He sat in the passenger seat of an older-model, midnight-blue sedan beside his partner Officer Holland. The unmarked police car groaned to a stop in front of Mr. Hardy's house. It was a quiet, rainy Sunday morning.

"Those brakes sound like me trying to get out of bed in the morning," laughed Detective Taylor. Officer Holland was to take Detective Taylor's place when he retired at the end of the year. He looked at his superior. He wasn't sure how to respond, so he just nodded and smiled.

Detective Taylor took in a deep breath. "That's some house," he said as he unfastened his seatbelt, looking out the window.

"Yes, sir," Officer Holland nodded again, arching his gargantuan furry eyebrows. His eyebrows had always been large and furry. As a kid, he would stand in the mirror raising his eyebrows until they touched his hairline. He could also wiggle them, so it looked like two furry caterpillars chasing each other.

Detective Taylor climbed out of the police car, quickly hopping over a puddle. He gazed out at Mr. Hardy's perfectly manicured lawn. His yard looked like it belonged on the cover of *Better Homes and Gardens* magazine. Not only was the lawn immaculate, but perfectly trimmed hedges framed the front of the house, and islands of colorful flowers dotted the yard.

Connecting to the side of the house was a six-foot-high, wooden privacy fence—which Detective Taylor suspected encircled the entire backyard.

The front door burst open, and a man who looked like an egg, dressed in a forest green suit, ran down the sidewalk toward them.

"Thank God you're here!" His hand swooped upward, opening the smallest umbrella the officers had ever seen.

"Mr. Hardy?" inquired Detective Taylor, signaling with his hands for the rapidly approaching man to slow down.

"Yes. Yes. I'm so sorry. It's just that on *Law & Order* they say that the first twelve hours in a kidnapping are the most crucial."

"We understand," said Detective Taylor, taking control of the conversation. "I'm Detective Taylor and this is Officer Holland. We are here to help you, but we'll need you to calm down a little so we can help you."

"Yes. Yes. I apologize," said Mr. Hardy, as he pulled a small, colorful handkerchief from his pocket and wiped the rain from his forehead. "It's just… I've *never* been the victim of such a heinous crime."

"I understand," said Detective Taylor, giving Mr. Hardy a reassuring smile. "How about showing Officer Holland and I where the crime took place."

"Of course officers. Follow me," said Mr. Hardy, beckoning them toward his house. "Oh, and please remove your shoes. I just had my carpets cleaned."

~~o~o~o~~

Detective Taylor and Officer Holland followed Mr. Hardy up the sidewalk and into the house. The living room was just as Officer Holland had imagined it would be. A beautiful ornate sofa covered with plastic. A wide-screen TV mounted to the wall, surrounded by shelves filled with dozens of pictures of Mr. Hardy and a brown and white dog, with whom he could only assume was Mr. Binxley. Above the sofa hung a ginormous painting of Mr. Binxley laying on a massive purple pillow with golden fringe and tassels.

Mr. Hardy saw Officer Holland notice the painting. His chest heaved. "Regal, isn't he? Absolutely regal."

"Stunning," replied Officer Holland, once again not sure how to respond.

Detective Taylor sighed. "Where was your dog—I'm sorry, I mean Mr. Binxley—when you noticed he was missing?"

"In his master suite of course," he gestured toward the hallway. "This way."

The officers followed Mr. Hardy through the house to Mr. Binxley's room. Again, Officer Holland already had some idea as to what the room was going to look like, and he wasn't disappointed. The room was painted a baby blue with white trim around the windows and floorboards. The ceiling was white, with wispy blue clouds. Baby-blue shelves lined the walls, filled with trophies and ribbons and porcelain figurines of Cavalier King Charles Spaniels involved in various activities.

A huge dog bed filled with pillows and chew toys was nestled into a corner, and across the room, in the opposite corner, sat a small crate, designed to look like a miniature hotel. A chandelier dangled from the center of the ceiling. Officer Holland had to duck under it to cross the room.

"This is quite the room," said Detective Taylor slowly turning in a circle.

"It's quaint," smiled Mr. Hardy, "but it's home."

"Is that Mozart?" asked Officer Holland, pointing to a set of Bose speakers.

"Oh yes. Mr. Binxley loves all the classics, Mozart, Chopin… he insists on listening to Bach for dinner."

"Okay…. When was the last time you saw Mr. Binxley?" asked Detective Taylor, pulling out a notebook and pen from his sports coat.

"I left here at nine o'clock to make my usual Starbucks run, and when I came back home…," his bottom lip began to quiver. "…Mr. Binxley was gone."

Detective Taylor nodded… and pursed his lips. Twenty-five years on the police force, one more year till he retired, and now he was investigating the disappearance of a dog….

"Are you sure Mr. Binxley didn't run out when you opened the door? You know that happens a lot more often than you would think," suggested Officer Holland.

"Yes, I'm sure. I *always* close his bedroom door when I leave. Plus, I found this on the floor." He picked up a blue collar covered with diamonds. An engraved tag in the shape of a bone that read "Tri State Champion, Mr. Binxley" dangled from the front.

"Was Mr. Binxley chipped?" asked Officer Holland, as he began taking pictures of the crime scene.

"Indeed not! I would never hurt Mr. Binxley or betray his trust by permanently scarring him with a tracking device. It's simply unimaginable."

"Okay…," sighed Officer Holland. "Just a thought."

"His *necklace* has a tracking chip and a QR code, that if you scan it, it gives his phone number and address."

"Except—you're holding the collar…," pointed out Detective Taylor

"We prefer to call it a *neck* accessory," corrected Mr. Hardy.

Detective Taylor turned his head, cracking his neck. "His *collar* is in your hand. You're also contaminating evidence."

"Oh!" exclaimed Mr. Hardy as he dropped the collar onto the floor. "Sorry."

Detective Taylor bit his tongue. "Can you show me where the dognapper broke in?" he asked with a measured tone.

"Yes," said Mr. Hardy, oblivious to the detective's annoyance. "He came in through the kitchen. Follow me."

Detective Taylor peppered Mr. Hardy with questions as they walked through the house.

"Did you have any enemies that might want to steal Mr. Binxley?"

"*Everyone* was jealous of Mr. Binxley. The *Paw News* described his incredible ascent in the show dog world as '*unparalleled* and *meteoric*.' Mr. Binxley has won some of the most prestigious dog shows in the world…. He is worth a fortune."

"But," paused Detective Taylor, "it's not like someone could sell him—the show dog world is quite small and close-knit. It's not like they could steal him and then compete with him…."

"No," agreed Mr. Hardy. "They cannot do anything without his papers, which are hidden in an envelope under my—"

"Your desk," interrupted Detective Taylor. He knew by the look on Mr. Hardy's face that he had guessed correctly.

Mr. Hardy raced out of the kitchen, through the house, flinging open the door to his office. Detective Taylor stood in the doorway and watched as Mr. Hardy wiggled his egg-shaped body beneath his desk.

"They're gone!" he yelled out. "Mr. Binxley's papers are gone!"

"I know," said Detective Taylor apologetically. He reached down and helped Mr. Hardy as he struggled to his feet.

"How… how did you know?" asked Mr. Hardy, producing a miniature lint roller from inside his jacket. Officer Holland nearly choked trying to contain his laughter.

"When you've been doing this as long as I have," said Detective Taylor, "you become a pretty good predictor of human behavior."

He smiled sympathetically at Mr. Hardy. "Let's go take a look at where he broke in."

Detective Taylor knelt in front of the kitchen door. He could see pieces of splintered wood and chips of blue paint on the tile floor. He slipped on a pair of white latex gloves and gingerly opened the door, examining the door frame and what had once been the locking mechanism.

He looked up at Mr. Hardy. "It looks like the thief used a crowbar. People think they're safe with a bolt lock, but a professional thief can force their way into a door like this in a matter of seconds."

He stepped outside onto the porch and took in his surroundings. The backyard was completely fenced in. Once the intruder was in the backyard, he would have plenty of time to break in. No one would be able to see what he was doing.

"Does your gate have a lock?" asked Detective Taylor, pointing at a gate that led to the driveway.

"Not a real lock. You pull down on the lever, and that's it. I used to have a lock on it, but it became a nuisance."

"I see. So the intruder came through the gate, broke into the back door, grabbed the paperwork, and then grabbed Mr. Binxley—and most likely exited the same way. I'll have Officer Holland dust for prints… but most likely, this was well planned, and our thief wore gloves."

Detective Taylor wrote down a few more notes while Officer Holland dusted for prints.

"We'll run the prints by the lab and check with the neighbors to see if they saw anything," Detective Taylor said handing him his card. "If you see anything, hear anything, think of anything, give me a call."

"Thank you," replied Mr. Hardy quietly, saddened that they hadn't found any earth-shattering clues. "I will."

He waved to the officers as they drove off and then quietly turned and stared into his living room, his heart heavy.

Everything seemed so empty. Suddenly, he felt very alone.

3
NO CASE TOO BIG, NO CASE TOO SMALL

Mr. Hardy reached for the remote and turned on the TV. He needed some noise, a distraction, anything to take him away from his horrid thoughts.

"And our very own, world-famous Livingston detectives, Ava Clarke and Carol Miller, who recently helped capture a dangerous clan of thieves using the underground...."

Mr. Hardy raced up to the television, pressing the volume-up button on the remote with his thumb. He stared at the screen, completely absorbed by the two girls dressed in matching black hoodies.

A scrawler across the bottom of the screen read, "Ava Clarke, Livingston Detective." A young girl with light brown hair and purple highlights smiled brightly at the camera.

"Carol and I have actually chased criminals all over the world—Italy, France.... Ahem, so far just Italy and France, but we are looking at Greenland, something about it being covered in ice and not actually being green doesn't sit well with me."

A picture of the girls standing by the Arno River in Italy where they'd rescued a man that had been kidnapped appeared on the screen. The next picture showed Carol at Camp Oakwood, in their hometown of Livingston. She was whipping what looked like two golf balls connected by a short piece of rope through the air.

"Oh, interesting. And what are we seeing in this picture?" inquired the woman reporter.

"That picture was taken right here in Livingston in Camp Oakwood. I'm teaching a class on how to throw a bola. Ava's father brought it back from his trip to the Amazon. He said the indigenous people use it there to hunt for food."

"Fascinating. *Very* intimidating," said the reporter.

Carol nodded enthusiastically, her reddish-brown ponytail bobbing up and down. "I plan to use it to hunt for criminals," she said, turning to the camera, arching a well-manicured eyebrow.

The scrawler on the bottom of the TV screen read, "Carol Miller, Livingston Detective, Bola Thrower."

"Do you have any *new* cases you want to tell us about?" asked the reporter.

"Nothing yet," smiled Carol. "But, if you have a case that needs to be solved, give us a call."

"No case too big, no case too small," Ava added as she leaned into the microphone.

The camera zoomed in on the reporter. "Well, there you have it, Livingston. No case too big or too small…. Ava and Carol, Livingston's own dynamic duo, are ready to help you out."

Behind the woman's left shoulder, Ava's hands crept up into the frame. She used her fingers to indicate the digits to her phone number.

Mr. Hardy trembled with excitement. This is who he needed! The Ava and Carol Detective Agency!

4
A HAIRY SITUATION

Ava raised her hand to knock on Mr. Hardy's door, when the door suddenly flew open.

"You're here!" Mr. Hardy squealed. "Thank you so much for coming on such short notice! I literally just saw you on TV."

"Really?" asked Ava, delighted. "How did my hair look? I'm trying someth—"

"You're welcome, Mr. Hardy," said Carol, stepping in front of Ava, offering him her hand. "We're glad to help."

"Wonderful," exclaimed Mr. Hardy, awkwardly grabbing the tips of Carol's fingers and shaking them. "Please, come in, come in," he said, ushering them inside.

Carol paused in the living room, staring at the dozens of pictures of Mr. Binxley lining the walls. *This man really loves his dog.*

"Mr. Binxley is beautiful," smiled Ava, "and *extremely* photogenic. If you don't mind me asking, what kind of product do you use on his hair? It's so hard to get that natural, healthy shine."

"Ava," fumed Carol, "the case! We're here for the case."

"It's called multitasking," said Ava emphatically. "Besides," she frowned, "I'm trying to learn more about Mr. Binxley."

Carol gave Ava the stink-eye and then turned to Mr. Hardy. "Could you please show us where the crime took place?"

"Certainly," nodded Mr. Hardy, gesturing toward the back of the house. "Mr. Binxley's suite is this way."

"Suite?" Ava mouthed to no one in particular.

"Did you contact the police, Mr. Hardy?" asked Carol as she followed closely behind him.

"Yes. I spoke to Detective Taylor and Officer...," he clicked his fingers and knotted his eyebrows, trying to remember. "Oh yes, Officer Holland."

"If you contacted the police, why did you call us?" asked Carol, confused.

Mr. Hardy's face flushed. "Well... honestly, I had the feeling that this wasn't going to be a high-priority case." He emphasized the words 'high priority' by making air quotes with his fingers. "Not that they weren't thorough, or professional. I could just tell that...," he paused, trying not to break down. "You have to realize... Mr. Binxley is like my child."

"We understand," smiled Ava, patting him reassuringly on the shoulder. "We'll make sure that your case gets *top priority*."

"Thank you so much," he smiled, looking more relieved. "Here it is, Mr. Binxley's suite."

Carol stepped into the room, slowly turning and taking in all of the details, just like Detective Taylor had done. Satisfied, she pulled out her phone and began taking pictures of the entire room from floor to ceiling.

While Carol snapped away, Ava opened a voice recording app on her phone and began to interview Mr. Hardy.

"April twenty-third 11:47 a.m. Mr. Hardy, what type of shampoo and conditioner did you use on—"

"Ava Clarke!" said Carol sharply.

"Fine," sighed Ava. "Mr. Hardy, when did you realize that Mr. Binxley was missing?"

"Well, I walked to Starbucks, like I do each morning at about nine o'clock, and when I returned home… Mr. Binxley…," he held his hand to his mouth. "Well, he usually barks and barks until I open the door to his room."

Carol shot Ava a look. She knew what she was thinking.

"Mr. Hardy, do you walk to Starbucks every day?" asked Ava gently.

"Yes," he nodded. "It's my morning routine."

"*Every* morning, at the same time?" asked Ava.

"Yes…, their Frappuccinos are to die for," he said, looking at Ava with a *why are you asking me this?* expression.

"It's true," she agreed. "Great... now I want a decaf latte." Carol's sigh of exasperation traveled across the room. Ava bit her lip and continued questioning Mr. Hardy. "And how long would you say you are gone each morning?"

"About thirty minutes."

"And did you ever notice anything suspicious, or different?" continued Ava.

"Like what?" he asked, confused.

"A new car in the neighborhood... perhaps the feeling of being followed. Maybe someone other than the regular crowd you see at Starbucks every day. Anything...?"

"No," he said, pausing to think. "I don't think so. I'm sorry," he frowned. "I'm horrible at this."

"No, *please* don't apologize. Most people's lives are made up of routines and they rarely pay attention to their surroundings. Their brains simply filter it out as noise. They're not highly trained observers like us."

"I guess you're right," said Mr. Hardy, as if this were the first time the thought had ever crossed his mind. "I've been walking to Starbucks for nearly three years now.... I *really* don't pay that much attention."

"Thieves love predictability," explained Carol. "After just a few days of observing you, they know the following," Carol held up her hand and ticked off the reasons on her fingers. "One, you leave at nine o'clock every morning. Two, you are gone for at least thirty minutes. Three, you take the same route every day."

"Since you take the same route," added Ava, "they can easily follow you, and they can easily avoid running into you."

"Plus, they know you go to Starbucks every day," resumed Carol. "They could have an accomplice at Starbucks. When you walked in, the accomplice could have sent a text to the thief, letting them know it was safe to break in."

"I am confused about one thing: Why steal Mr. Binxley?" said Ava. "Don't they have to show special breeding documents and ownership papers at dog shows? Our friend Kelly breeds Chihuahuas and has to have all kinds of paperwork."

"Yes, you do. The shows require his pedigree documentation, his inoculation records—"

"Exactly," whispered Carol. "So without those, the thief wouldn't be able to—"

"The papers were...," Mr. Hardy took a deep breath, "...stolen as well."

"Okay, but isn't Mr. Binxley well known?" said Carol. "It's not like I could just show up with him at a dog show and claim ownership."

"Oh yes," said Mr. Hardy proudly. "He's won over a quarter-million dollars, and this is only his third year competing."

"A quarter-million?" asked Ava, her jaw dropping.

"Yes, there is big money in dog shows and breeding, and then there are sponsors…. Mr. Binxley was just on the cover of *Modern Dog* magazine, and rumor has it, he's going to be one of the judges' favorites at the Westminster Kennel Club show in New York. He's becoming quite famous."

"So…," said Ava, thinking out loud. "If Mr. Binxley is kidnapped, he can't be entered into any competitions because he would instantly be recognized. You can't really sell him; he's worth a fortune, but he makes his money through competing…."

"So, what's the thief's motive?" asked Carol, continuing Ava's line of thought. Suddenly her eyebrows arched upward.

Ava knew this meant she had an idea… or gas. She was hoping it was an idea.

"Would a competitor risk kidnapping Mr. Binxley to get him out of the game? You know, so they have a better chance to win?"

Ava gave Carol a look of approval. "Great question, big brain."

"I suppose," he said slowly. "Us dog people are an… interesting bunch. Last year Simone, a beautiful standard poodle, was stolen. Sir Garland, the owner, was heartbroken. He offered huge rewards, hired a private investigator, but after six months, he finally gave up."

"Wow, that's really sad," said Ava.

"Don't worry, this story has a happy ending," smiled Mr. Hardy wanly. "You see, the thief waited until Sir Garland had given up searching. Although… I'm quite sure he never really gave up, if you know what I mean."

The girls nodded as one.

"And then… he began showing 'Belle' as his own."

"Wait," said Carol, holding up her hand. "First, you said they had to have the proper paperwork, and second, wouldn't someone recognize Simone?"

"Yes, the thief had expertly forged documents, and he dyed Simone's beautiful ivory fur black."

"So… how did he get caught?" inquired Ava.

"Karma," he smiled.

"Karma," exclaimed Ava nodding her head. "It'll get you."

"Yes it will," agreed Mr. Hardy, "but I'm talking about Karma De La Torre. She's a famous judge," added Mr. Hardy, seeing the confused look on the girls' faces.

"She had better be, with a name like that. Karma De La Torre," repeated Ava dramatically.

"Please continue," smiled Carol placing her hand over Ava's mouth before she could belt out another "Karma De La Torre."

"The thief entered 'Belle' into a prestigious Las Vegas dog show," continued Mr. Hardy. "Unfortunately for him, Karma De La Torre—the head judge—became ill with food poisoning, and an alternate judge had to take her place."

"Sir Garland," smiled Carol.

"Exactly," said Mr. Hardy pointing a stubby finger at Carol. "You're as quick as a whip. As soon as Simone saw Sir Garland, she bolted across the stage. She immediately sat at his feet, raised her paw, and tapped on his pocket twice. This was Simone's way of asking for a treat. He reached into his pocket and placed a treat on Simone's nose, then snapped his fingers. Simone tossed the treat into the air with her cute little snout and caught it. That's when he knew for sure it was Simone. The thief tried to run away… only to trip and fall into a waste can filled with… dog poop. And that, my girls," he cocked an eyebrow, "is a smell that lingers."

"Okayyyy…. On that note," said Carol, "I'm gonna need a list of all the competitors in your division. Highlight anyone on the list whom you would suspect."

"Including anyone you've had an argument with or would have a lot to gain from Mr. Binxley's disappearance," added Ava.

"You got it," said Mr. Hardy, feeling better that he was actively involved in the investigation.

Carol swiped her finger across her phone, looking at the array of pictures she had taken. "I think we're about done here...." Carol paused tilting her head from side to side, looking at the chandelier. Something had caught her eye; it looked like a wispy piece of spider web. She moved closer. Hanging from the bottom of the crystal was a piece of human hair, caught in the golden clasp.

"What is it?" asked Ava.

"A hair," smiled Carol, gesturing toward a wavy piece of dark brown hair. "Mr. Hardy, has anyone else been in this room besides you?" she inquired.

"No, not for a long time.... Well...," he stopped himself, "...except for the two police officers."

Carol reached into her navy-blue backpack that she had converted into a miniature investigative lab. She removed a pair of white latex gloves, a small sheet of white paper, a white glassine envelope, and a pair of tweezers.

"Oils—micro debris—on our fingers can contaminate the evidence," offered Ava in response to the confused look on Mr. Hardy's face. "There are very important procedures that have to be followed, not to contaminate evidence."

Carol pulled the gloves on, then gently removed the hair from the chandelier with a pair of tweezers. She placed the hair onto the piece of white paper, folded the paper several times, and placed the hair into a small glassine envelope. She then placed the evidence in a larger envelope, then sealed, dated, and labeled it.

"Wow, you guys are thorough," said Mr. Hardy, clearly impressed. "Do you think the hair is from the thief?"

"It could be," said Carol. "We want to collect every tiny bit of evidence we can. Sometimes it's the smallest clue that catches the crook."

"We can get a lot of information from a single hair. We can also tell if the hair was dyed a different color or if it's synthetic, like from a wig. We can even tell the ethnicity," added Ava.

"Speaking of hair, may I collect a hair sample from you, Mr. Hardy?" asked Carol. "I'm pretty sure the hair isn't yours, but I'll need to make sure."

"Certainly!" Without a warning, Mr. Hardy reached up and plucked a hair from the top of his head. Ava winced and imagined a high-pitched *doink* sound as the hair was pulled. "Here," he said, offering the hair to Carol.

"One second," laughed Carol as she retrieved another evidence envelope. She placed his hair in a small envelope, then placed it in a larger envelope, dated it, and wrote a brief description onto the bag. She also collected a hair sample from Mr. Binxley's bed.

While Carol secured the evidence in her bag, Ava continued asking Mr. Hardy questions.

"Besides the paperwork, was anything else stolen?" asked Ava.

"Not that I can tell. Nothing else seemed to be disturbed," he replied.

"Aves," interrupted Carol, "I'm pretty sure the thief wore gloves... but I'm going to dust the doorknob for prints, just in case he got sloppy."

"Enjoy," said Ava as she stepped into the hallway, flicking on the lights.

Carol crouched at the door and removed a small jar of white powder and a soft-bristled brush. She gently rolled the brush between her hands a few times, causing the soft white bristles to flair out. Then ever so gently, she placed the tip of the brush into the white powder and gently coated the doorknob.

Ava crouched beside her and, using the flashlight app on her phone, illuminated the doorknob. Carol swiped to her magnifying app on her phone and inspected the knob.

"Anything?" asked Mr. Hardy excitedly.

"There are a couple partial prints," said Carol as she slowly rotated the knob, "but… I'm pretty sure they're going to turn out to be yours."

Carol grabbed a strip of thick clear tape and carefully placed it over the partial prints. Ava held a black piece of cardboard—the size of an index card—out for her to place the tape on.

Immediately, the partial prints came into view. Carol inspected them for a moment, then placed them in an envelope.

"Not much to go on," she sighed looking at the smudged prints, "but I'll know better once I get them under the microscope."

"We're gonna need a set of your fingerprints Mr. Hardy, so I can compare the prints from the door to yours."

"Certainly," said Mr. Hardy as he followed Carol back into Mr. Binxley's suite.

"This will be much easier," smiled Carol. She removed a square of white cardboard and an inkless fingerprint pad from her investigative kit.

"Relax," smiled Ava seeing the apprehensive look on Mr. Hardy's face. "It's a special formula that you can wipe off with a tissue. No staining."

"Thank goodness," replied Mr. Hardy still looking doubtful as he tentatively held out his hand.

Moments later, Carol had a complete set of Mr. Hardy's fingerprints.

"Okay," said Ava. "I think we are finished with this room for now. Mr. Hardy... where did the intruder break in?"

"My kitchen. He broke the lock on my kitchen door. Detective Taylor said he used a crowbar to pry the door open."

Carol nodded. "Simple, but effective."

She followed Mr. Hardy and Ava down the hall, through the den, and into the kitchen. Carol went to work right away. Kneeling, she began taking pictures of the door and the broken door frame with her phone.

"Geez," whispered Ava, "whoever did this really hates doors."

"If they'd been observant," said Carol, pointing to a window above the kitchen sink, "they could have just climbed in."

Ava looked at the window Carol was describing. Sure enough, the window was open a good six inches, the ledge lined with various potted plants.

"Maybe they're claustrophobic," offered Ava as she put on a pair of latex gloves. "Or very large."

Ava pulled out an evidence envelope and collected a few blue paint chips that had fallen to the ground. "Coral blue," she said with a smile. "Beautiful choice."

"Thank you," Mr. Hardy smiled. "It reminds me of the ocean. It's Mr. Binxley and my favorite place to vacation."

"Okay…," said Carol, raising her eyebrows. She pushed the kitchen door open and stood on the porch, surveying the yard. "This fence is great for privacy… but also great for anyone who wants to break into your house unseen."

"We've *never* had any problems in this neighborhood," said Mr. Hardy. "Every once in a while, a house gets toilet papered… but nothing like this."

Ava squeezed past Carol and began walking along the brick sidewalk.

"Wait!" called out Mr. Hardy. "I'll get my umbrella."

"That's okay," laughed Ava, pulling up her hood. "I'll be fine. It's barely raining."

She followed the brick sidewalk to the gate. A simple lever was all that kept the gate secured.

"No lock on this gate," she said, depressing the lever and opening the gate. "And…," she paused midsentence, "…there is a shoeprint in front of the gate! Mr. Hardy," Ava called out, "can you come here for a moment?"

"What is it?" he asked, hurrying over to Ava.

She pointed at the shoeprint, still fresh from the morning rain. "Do you have any shoes that match that sole?"

Mr. Hardy bent over to study the shoeprint, then shook his head.

"No… I can't say that I do. All my shoes are loafers… and I wear a size seven shoe…. This looks like size… ginormous!"

"I was pretty sure that our thief was a man, but this pretty much seals the deal. Not many women have a foot that big."

Carol appeared beside them, setting her detective kit on the ground. "A shoeprint! Great find, Ava."

"Thank you, Big Brain. They call me the shoeprint whisperer," said Ava while looking up at Mr. Hardy.

"They call you weirdo—now get the cardboard borders."

"How do you expect me to work under these conditions?" Ava fumed.

"I ask myself the same question daily," said Carol as she removed a bowl and filled it with white powder from her detective kit. She opened a bottle of water and slowly mixed it in with the powder until it had the consistency of liquidy paste.

"Plaster of Paris," commented Carol, seeing the confused look on Mr. Hardy's face.

"Leave it to the French to come up with something so amazing," said Mr. Hardy.

"The Egyptians actually created it about nine thousand years ago. Its actual name is calcium sulphate hemihydrate."

"Carol has a close relationship with Wikipedia," smiled Ava as she removed four strips of cardboard from the investigative kit. She poured a little oil onto a cotton ball. Then she coated one side of the cardboard border to keep the plaster of Paris from sticking to the border.

She carefully placed the border around the footprint and held them in place as Carol poured the white, gluey liquid onto the footprint.

"The shoeprint has officially been framed," smiled Ava. "It's also how we make cookies at home."

"I'm curious," said Mr. Hardy as he crouched over to watch the girls. "Why are you making a mold of a shoeprint?"

"A shoeprint can tie the suspect to the scene of the crime," explained Carol. "For example, when we catch whoever is behind this—"

"And we will," interjected Ava.

"Once we catch him," said Carol, starting again, "we can match this shoeprint with his shoes. We can even take soil samples from his shoes and compare them to your soil. It's just another way of saying the bad guy was definitely at the scene of the crime."

"Fascinating… you two are amazing!"

"All right," said Carol, inspecting her work once more. "It's going to take about an hour for the cast to dry."

"May I see your umbrella?" Ava asked Mr. Hardy.

"Certainly," he said handing it to her.

Ava placed the umbrella on the ground and leaned it so it shielded the footprint from the rain. "Perfect," she smiled.

"But that's my—"

"We need you to leave it right there," said Ava crisply. "We need to catch the thief, right?" Mr. Hardy looked distraught but nodded. "We can't do that with sloppy evidence collection."

"Alright," said Carol, snapping off her latex gloves. "We're going to head back to The Lair to analyze the clues. We'll be back in an hour or so to grab the cast."

"Thank you so much," smiled Mr. Hardy. "I truly appreciate everything." His eyes flickered to his umbrella.

"Not a worry, Mr. Hardy," said Carol as she packed up her detective kit. "Call us immediately if you need us. Otherwise, we'll see you soon!"

"Oh, I sent you a text," Ava told Mr. Hardy as they walked toward their bikes. "It's my email address. Send me the persons-of-interest list and a couple pictures of Mr. Binxley, as soon as you can!"

"I'll do that right now," said Mr. Hardy as he watched the girls ride away.

5
THE LAIR

The Lair was Ava and Carol's secret headquarters, hidden in the shadowy, recesses of Ava's parent's house. In the basement. Right next to the laundry room. (Don't judge.) Ava's father, a famous microbiologist, had helped them convert Ava's game room into an incredible crime lab. The sign on the door read, "Epic sleuthing in progress. Do not disturb." Underneath the sign was a smaller handwritten sign that read, "Unless you have brownies or cookies," and an even smaller sign that read, "And then you may proceed."

Carol sat on a wooden stool behind a large white table. Beakers, test tubes, jars filled with colorful powders and liquids, a laptop, and a powerful microscope that plugged into her computer sat atop the table.

On the other side of the lab, Ava sat at her wobbly, hand-me-down desk, fingers flying across her keyboard, grabbing the crime scene photos Carol had uploaded to the cloud. The printer whirred to life as she began printing the images from Mr. Hardy's house. Grabbing a fistful of magnets, she began arranging the images on the crime board—a large magnetic whiteboard that stood in the center of the room.

Grabbing a dry-erase marker, she wrote the words "Crime Scene" above the images. She then added the date, location, and time the pictures were taken. At the top of the board, she drew a timeline, to help keep track of the events and when they happened. She then drew another column and wrote the word "Suspects" at the top.

Suspects, thought Ava. She ran over to her laptop and brought up her emails. *Perfect.* Sitting at the top of her inbox was an email from Mr. Hardy with an attachment. She opened the attachment and clicked "Print."

"Got the list of suspects," yelled Ava across the room.

"Awesome," replied Carol as she snapped on a pair of latex gloves. She reached into her investigative kit and retrieved the hair samples she'd collected. Using a pair of tweezers, she carefully secured the hair labeled "Mr. Hardy" onto a glass slide and slid it under the microscope.

Slowly adjusting the viewer, she changed the magnification from 400 to 1,000. Viewed at a thousand times its normal size, the hair looked like a scaly roach leg. Hair definitely wasn't silky and smooth.

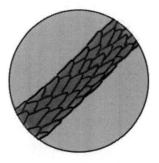

Carol's microscope was connected to her laptop, enabling her to take screenshots of the evidence. She made a few slight adjustments on the microscope, then printed a photo of the hair sample. Next, while using the software that came with the microscope, she saved the image to a folder named "Hardy Hair" on the cloud.

She then switched slides, repeating the process, this time viewing the strand of hair she'd found in the chandelier. The hair was dark brown, the color of coffee, and somewhat curly. And just like Mr. Hardy's hair, since it had been pulled out, it contained a tiny bit of skin tissue at the root. That tiny bit of tissue was incredibly important because it contained the person's DNA.

"Got you," she whispered.

She adjusted the microscope, and once she had a clear image, she pressed the print button. She also uploaded the picture to the "Hardy" folder and named the file "Suspect Hair."

Ava was busy reading through the list of suspects when her phone vibrated. She grabbed the phone off her desk, glancing down at the screen. "It's Mr. Hardy," she called out to Carol.

Carol immediately jumped up from her table and ran over. Ava tapped the speaker button so they could both listen.

"Hi, Mr. Hardy—" Ava had barely gotten the words out of her mouth when Mr. Hardy began talking excitedly. She put him on speaker so Carol could hear.

"A man called!" he said breathlessly. "He said that he had Mr. Binxley, and that if I wanted to see him alive again, I would have to give him ten thousand dollars in cash."

"Ten thousand dollars?!" exclaimed Carol.

"Yes! What do I do?"

"One moment," said Carol, closing her eyes, thinking. "Mr. Hardy, did you tell him you would pay him?"

"Of course I'll pay him! I'll do anything for Mr. Binxley," he replied.

"When, and how is he expecting the money?" asked Carol.

"He said he is going to call me back with the details in an hour. I tried to keep him on the phone as long as I could—you know, so you can trace the call. You know, like in the movies?"

"Uhm, thank you… but it doesn't really work that way."

"It doesn't?" he asked, feeling foolish.

"I'll explain when we get there," said Carol softly. "We're on our way right now. Please don't do anything until we get there. Okay?"

"Yes! Yes! Please hurry."

"We're on our way, Mr. Hardy," said Ava, ending the call.

"Pack up—we've got to rock and roll!" said Carol.

The girls grabbed their mobile investigation kits, slung them over their shoulders, and jumped onto their bikes. They pedaled furiously, knowing that they didn't have a second to spare. They needed to help Mr. Hardy plan a response. One mistake and Mr. Binxley could be gone forever.

6
THE RANSOM

The girls let themselves in through the gate, then hid their bikes in Mr. Hardy's backyard.

"Thank goodness you're here!" huffed Mr. Hardy as he stepped onto the back porch. "He's calling me back in forty-five minutes."

"Okay," said Carol, holding up her hands. "That gives us plenty of time. He's asking for ten thousand dollars. Do you have that much in the bank?"

"You're kidding, right? Of course I have that much money in the bank—have you seen my loafers?"

"I'm not really into shoes—"

"Or deodorant," added Ava.

"But I surmise from your answer that they are expensive, and that you have the money," continued Carol, ignoring Ava.

Mr. Hardy confirmed with a nod.

"Okay," said Carol, "here's the plan. My guess is he's going to be watching you closely. He wants to know if he can trust you. I want you to drive straight to the bank and withdraw ten thousand dollars. We want him to feel secure that you are doing everything he tells you to do. Once you have the money, come straight home." Carol glanced at her phone. "You have thirty-eight minutes. Do you bank at Charter?"

"Yes," answered Mr. Hardy, somewhat confused. "Why?"

"Mr. Charter is a close personal friend. I'm going to call him and give him a heads-up as to the situation. That way we can get you in and out of the bank as quickly as possible. He'll also be able to record the serial numbers of many of the bills."

Mr. Hardy looked at the girls, his face filled with worry. "What if I give him the money and...."

"Mr. Hardy," said Carol, patting his shoulder. "This is what we do best. It's why you hired us. Now please... we don't have much time!"

Mr. Hardy nodded, grabbed his keys, and dashed out the door.

The girls peeked through the curtains, watching as Mr. Hardy pulled away. Fifteen seconds later, an older-model gray Nissan Versa passed by.

Ava looked at Carol and raised her eyebrows. "Are you thinking what I'm thinking?"

Carol nodded. "It's a good chance that was the thief." She grabbed her phone and called Mr. Charter, the bank manager, and explained the situation. When she finished the call, she hung up and looked at Ava. "Fingers crossed Mr. Hardy takes our advice."

7
THE GIRLS SET A TRAP

Mr. Hardy returned home—and with only two minutes to spare, nearly giving the girls a heart attack. Sweat streamed down his face as he rushed through the front door. "I got it... I got the money...," he panted.

"Perfect," said Ava. "He should be—"

Mr. Hardy's phone rang before she could finish speaking.

"It says *unknown*," whispered Mr. Hardy excitedly.

"That's gotta be him. Answer it, and turn it to speaker," whispered Carol.

He nodded, his hand shaking as he took the call.

"Hello," he said, his voice quavering.

Ava held her phone next to Mr. Hardy's phone, recording the conversation. A creepy, deep, electronic voice began speaking. Carol's eyes met Ava's. He was using voice-changing technology to disguise his voice.

"Do you have the money?"

"Yes," whispered Mr. Hardy, his voice barely audible.

"Was that a yes?" asked the deep voice.

"Yes," said Mr. Hardy more firmly. "I have the money."

"Do you know where Murphy's Bike Shop is located?"

"It's beside the new law office that's being built," whispered Carol into his ear.

"Yes, yes I do."

"Good. Listen closely. Next to the front door of Murphy's is a large green mailbox. Inside that mailbox you'll find a satchel. Put the money inside and walk away. *If*," he continued, "you try any tricks, or *if* you try to get the cops involved… well, let's just say Mr. Binxley is going to take a long, long nap. Understood?"

"Please, please don't hurt Mr. Binxley," Mr. Hardy cried out. "I understand!"

"I will be watching your every move! You have thirty minutes to make the drop. Understood?"

"Yes. Yes, I understand. But how am I going to get Mr. Binxley back?"

"As soon as I make sure that you've paid me my ten grand, then I'll tell you where you can pick up your mutt."

Mr. Hardy sucked his breath in hard. "How do… I know…."

"Look, *Milton*…," he spat out his name, as if he had taken a bite of a disgusting sandwich and he was spitting it out. Mr. Hardy's eyebrows shot up, surprised at hearing his name spoken this way. "Do we have a deal? Your dog's life depends on it!"

"Yes, sir, we have a deal," squeaked Mr. Hardy.

"Good boy," the man laughed evilly.

The phone went dead. Mr. Hardy's knees gave way, and he began to sob.

Ava knelt in front of him, grabbing his shoulders. "Mr. Hardy, you've got to be strong. Mr. Binxley is counting on you."

"You did a great job!" said Carol kindly. "Don't worry, we'll get Mr. Binxley back for you."

"He's nothing but a heartless coward," said Ava, fighting hard to keep the anger out of her voice.

Mr. Hardy wiped the tears away with the back of his hand and tightened his jaw.

"Wait," he said, hope suddenly filling his face. "Can't we track his phone call?"

"I can almost guarantee that he is using a burner phone," replied Carol, hating to put a damper on his excitement.

"A burner?" inquired Mr. Hardy.

"A burner is a cheap, prepaid, disposable phone. It's become super popular with criminals. They'll use it once or twice, shut it down, pull out the battery, and then throw it away. That way it can't be pinged or tracked back to them," said Carol.

"Oh, great," he said disappointedly. "Once we give him the money, we have to trust this guy to give us Mr. Binxley back?"

"No," smiled Carol, "but you do have to trust us to do our job."

"Plus," said Ava, "did you catch the way he called you Milton? It sounded very personal, like he knew you."

"I caught that too," said Carol. "I think that clue is definitely going to prove helpful."

Ava nodded. "I'm uploading a recording of the conversation to the cloud now."

"Okay, Mr. Hardy. I need you to pay *close* attention," said Carol.

"Okay," he whispered softly.

"Here's what we need you to do. Drive slowly and *directly* to Murphy's Bike Shop. Today is Murphy's Race for Cancer event, so the bike store will be closed for the day."

"...I'm certain that we can believe what he said—that he'll be watching you," added Ava.

Carol nodded in agreement. "Get out of your car, don't look around, and don't spook him. Take the money to the mailbox and do exactly what he said. Once you put the money in the satchel, go directly to your car and drive straight home. Stay here until you hear from us."

"Keep your phone close by, because things are going to happen very quickly!" added Ava.

Mr. Hardy stared at the girls for a moment. It was a lot to take in. "Okay," he nodded, setting his jaw. "Let's get Mr. Binxley!"

8
OPERATION DONUT

A dozen or so cars and pedestrians peppered Canal Street. The weather had cleared, and a slight breeze sent cottony blue clouds scurrying across the sky. Ava and Carol sat at a circular green table with a green umbrella outside Dillard's Donut Shack. From their vantage point, they had a clear view of Murphy's Bike Shop, which was about a hundred feet from where they sat.

To the casual observer, Ava and Carol looked like a couple girls enjoying the beautiful spring day, while devouring a box of donut holes. In reality, they had quickly converted the donut box into a cleverly devised surveillance device.

One side of the box contained the actual delicious donut holes, while the other half contained a section to hold an iPhone with a telescopic lens attached to it. They aligned the lens with the letter *O* that had been cut out of the box, allowing Ava to secretly film everything. It took a little fiddling, but after a few moments she was able to zoom in on Murphy's shop.

"I believe we should figure out a way to incorporate donuts into every investigation," said Ava, licking her fingers.

"Aves, here he comes," whispered Carol as a midnight blue Volvo with a "You Had Me at Woof" bumper sticker passed them. Mr. Hardy's car slowed to a stop in front of Murphy's Bike Shop.

"Right on time," smiled Ava as she grabbed a chocolate donut hole.

They watched Mr. Hardy climb out of his car and scurry over to the bike shop. He disappeared from view for a few seconds and then reappeared, walking briskly to his car. Without looking around, he climbed in and drove away.

"Kudos to him," said Ava through a mouthful of chocolate donut. "Great job."

"He did just what we asked," said Carol, studying Canal Street. Mr. Hardy had barely been gone a minute when she whispered, "Gray Nissan approaching—it looks like the same one from his neighborhood."

Ava slowly turned her head toward Carol, both girls in hyper-alert mode. She twisted the hidden camera toward the street and began recording as the gray Nissan Versa passed by. Sunlight reflected off the passenger window, making it difficult to see the driver.

"Connecticut license plates," whispered Ava.

Carol stood up and walked over to her bike, removing a small rectangular object from her jacket pocket.

"Here we go," smiled Carol. She walked her bike out to the sidewalk, then pretended to tie her shoe. Out of the corner of her eye, she watched a tall man, dressed in black jeans and a black hoodie, climb out of his car. The man paused and looked up and down the street for a few moments, then made his way toward Murphy's Bike Shop.

Carol hopped on her bike and checked Canal Street for oncoming traffic as Ava began a ten-second countdown.

Ten, nine, eight, seven….

Carol pedaled slowly down Canal Street, her heart pounding in her chest. When she reached the man's car, she quietly brought her bike to a stop. She could see the man, just twenty feet away, his back turned to her as he opened the green mailbox.

Carol quickly hopped off her bike and attached a rectangular object beneath the man's car. She stole a look at the man, who was just pulling the satchel of money out of the mailbox. Risking a quick glance behind her, she let go a sigh of relief as she saw Ava climbing onto her bike. She checked for cars and then darted out into the street, disappearing around the corner.

Ava pedaled down Canal Street, taking in deep breaths. Everything depended on her acting skills. As soon as she got close to the man's car, she hopped the curb with her bike, and then threw herself and the bike to the ground.

"Ooof!" she cried out. "Ow! Ow! Ow!"

The man had just opened the satchel of money and torn off the top of the envelope. *He's counting the money.*

Ava's plan was to make the man panic, so he would lead them to either Mr. Binxley or his hideout—she knew he wouldn't want a lot of attention directed toward him. "Ouch!" Ava cried out. "My bike, my donuts, my pride."

The man looked at her angrily. People were beginning to react to Ava as she lay on the sidewalk moaning. A young woman hurried toward her, to make sure she was okay.

Ava dragged herself across the sidewalk, moaning. "Oh, the pain!"

Frustrated, the man took another quick glance in the bag and then hurried off toward his car. Ava leaned against his car, using the car door to pull herself to her feet. She quickly turned the donut box, filming the interior.

"That's my car, kid!" growled the man, obviously annoyed by Ava's antics.

"Oh, I'm sorry, sir," said Ava, pushing herself off his car. "My tire must have hit the curb."

"Don't care," growled the man as he hurried past Ava. He quickly popped the trunk open and threw the satchel inside.

Ava leaned forward, filming the interior of his trunk with her donut box.

"Would you like a donut hole, sir? I've got powdered, chocolate, glazed…. Sir?"

The man ignored her barrage of questions. Slamming the trunk shut, he pushed past her and climbed into his car. "How *rude*," Ava cried out indignantly. The man ignored her, pulled away from the curb and drove off, heading toward Main Street.

"Are you okay?" asked a young woman in a New York Yankees cap.

"Yes, ma'am, thank you. I just can't hop curbs like I used to."

"Are you sure you're okay? You took quite a spill."

"I'm fine, thank you. I think the only thing hurt is my pride," laughed Ava.

The woman gave Ava a once-over and shook her head. "Ah, to be young and resilient."

Ava thanked the woman again, offered her a slightly flattened donut hole, and then rode back to the donut shack to rendezvous with Carol.

"Hurry, hurry!" Carol was waving her arm wildly at Ava. "What the heck were you doing back there?"

"A lady was just making sure I was—"

"Never mind," said Carol, waving away Ava's response, her attention completely devoted to the screen of her iPhone.

"You got him?" asked Ava excitedly.

"Yep."

Ava scooted beside Carol, and they watched live GPS updates of the suspect's car on Carol's phone.

Using strong magnets, Carol had attached an old, refurbished iPhone, running a location app, to the underside of the kidnapper's car. A little red arrow moved in real time, through the streets of Livingston. The kidnapper would unknowingly lead them right to his hideout.

9
THE CHASE

"Let's go!" urged Carol. "He's heading toward the Hawthorne Pines neighborhood in Concord."

"You had me at 'let's go,'" smiled Ava.

The girls hopped on their bikes, pedaling furiously, following the little red arrow like a carrot dangling off the end of a stick.

"I'm going to call Detective Taylor so he can meet us there!" yelled Ava. A clump of purple highlighted hair blew under her nose, giving her a purple mustache.

"Great!" Carol yelled back, trying to focus on the GPS signal while dodging potholes.

Holding on to the handlebars with one hand, Ava called the direct number Mr. Hardy had provided her, for Detective Taylor. After two rings, a gruff voice answered the phone.

"Detective Taylor speaking."

"Detective Taylor, this is Ava Clarke…," she panted.

"He stopped," Carol gasped. "I'm bringing up a Google satellite view of the neighborhood now."

Ava nodded her head excitedly. "Sorry about the interruption," she huffed. "I'm a good friend of Detective Edwards, and—"

"I know who you are," he laughed. "Are you okay? You seem winded."

"In hot pursuit, sir. We need backup. We know who kidnapped Mr. Binxley."

"What? How the heck?"

"Sir, he has the ransom money, there's nothing to stop him from disappearing with Mr. Binxley. He could take the money and run!"

"Ransom money? Ava, where are you?" asked Detective Taylor.

Ava guessed that he was probably scrambling through his house looking for his car keys.

"I'm about to send you a screenshot of our location on Google Maps," replied Ava.

"Okay, I'm on my way. Don't, and I repeat, *do not* engage the suspect."

Ava exhaled…. She was about to make a promise she knew she wouldn't keep. "I promise I won't *engage* the suspect."

Ava's phone vibrated. She swiped to the image she just received from Carol, then quickly texted it to Detective Taylor.

"Location is sent," said Ava.

A second later she heard a ding. "Got it," Detective Taylor replied. "I've alerted Officer Holland. Stay where you are. We'll be there in a few minutes."

"Yes, sir. And oh, Detective Taylor? We have *all* the evidence that you'll need."

Detective Taylor smiled to himself and shook his head. "I'm sure you do."

10
NOT SO FAST

Pedaling manically, Ava and Carol lowered their heads as the wind whipped around them. Trees and mailboxes were a blur as they whizzed by.

"GPS says we'll be there in two minutes," called out Carol.

"Thank goodness," said Ava, groaning. "My donut holes are about to rebel."

The girls raced through neighborhood after neighborhood, until they arrived at a long, winding driveway that snaked deep into a wooded lot.

"Uhm…," gulped Carol. "This looks like the beginning to a really bad movie."

Ava nodded. "I know," she burped. "Is my face green? It feels like my face is green."

"What should we do?" Carol glanced around anxiously. "The police will be here any minute…."

"Wait…? Find a place for me to vomit…? Either option works for me."

"What if he hurts Mr. Binxley—I mean, now that he has the money?" asked Carol, thinking out loud.

"That's not fair," moaned Ava. "You know I have a weak spot for animals. Alright, let's see if we can stall the guy till the police get here."

"Besides, the police will be here in two minutes, Aves—what could possibly go wrong between now and then?" encouraged Carol.

"Only one way to find out," said Ava, praying she wasn't going to puke.

Carol nodded as she began racing down the gravel driveway, leaving a plume of dust and flying rock. Ava pedaled furiously behind her. She slid to a stop as the driveway switched from gravel to asphalt. Moments later, Ava appeared beside her. Ava's lips were now a strange shade of green.

The man was just about to step inside the house when Ava yelled out to him. And then covered her mouth as she belched.

"Sir." *Belch*. "Hey, sir!"

The man's hood was down, revealing a mass of coffee-colored, curly brown hair. He had pale thin lips and a crooked nose that looked like he'd wound up on the wrong side of a fist a few times.

He turned and walked down two steps. His eyes narrowed. "I know you," he growled, pointing a finger at Ava. "You're the kid from the sidewalk."

"Yeah, thanks for your help. I ruined a perfectly good box of donuts because of you."

"He's so tall," whispered Carol out of the corner of her mouth.

The man began walking toward the girls, pointing an accusatory finger at Ava. "Why are you following me?"

"Do you want the truth?" asked Ava. "Or may I lie?"

"Depends," smiled the man evilly. "How do you feel about basements and *duct tape*?"

"That's my trigger word," said Carol, looking frantically at Ava. "That's my trigger word!" She began to back away slowly.

"Okay, okay," said Ava, holding up her hands. "We're tiny compared to you. We're just two twelve-year-old kids. We saw you grab something out of Mr. Murphy's mailbox. My dad works part-time at that store. We thought you were stealing something."

The man's face relaxed a tiny bit. "Oh that," he laughed. "Nah, Mr.… uh… Murphy left me some information. He…," the man paused, tilting his head. "What the heck?" he yelled as a midnight blue sedan followed by a police cruiser roared down the driveway.

"Oh that," smiled Ava, burping. "Yeah, I might have forgot about the part where we called the police."

As Ava talked, Carol's fingers slowly slipped inside her jacket, removing what looked like a piece of three-foot rope with a golf ball attached to each end. Ava had decorated the golf balls, painting them yellow and adding angry faces.

As the man turned to run, Carol whipped the bola above her head like a lasso. The man literally took two steps when Carol released the angry-faced bola. It whistled through the air and struck him behind the knees, wrapping around his legs like a python.

The man tripped and fell face forward with a loud "Ooof." He immediately rolled over, sat up kicking his legs in an effort to free himself, but only succeeded in kicking off one of his boots. In a flash, Detective Taylor and Officer Holland surrounded him.

"Ava Clarke, what does *do not engage* mean to you?" yelled Detective Taylor.

"From everything I've read, it has something to do with marriage... and I certainly would not marry this man."

Detective Taylor shook his head and sighed. "Do you want to tell me what's going on?" he asked, staring at the man sitting on the ground, ensnared by two angry faces.

"He's the guy who kidnapped Mr. Binxley... and we can prove it," Ava gave the thief the stink-eye.

"Whoa, whoa, whoa!" said the man as he threw up his hands. "Kidnapper? I think you have me confused with someone else."

"No," smiled Carol. "I'm quite sure you are *exactly* who we're looking for."

"I've never kidnapped a person in my life, I swear."

"How about dog-napped a person?" implored Ava.

"Or a dog," clarified Carol.

The man finished untangling his legs and then looked up at Detective Taylor. "I have no idea what these girls are talking about."

"Oh, I think you do," said Ava as she removed her phone from her jacket. "Here's the call that Mr. Hardy received this morning." Detective Taylor and Officer Holland listened intently to the recorded phone call.

"See," the man cried out, "that's not even my voice. He's got some deep, gurgly voice like Darth Vader."

Carol looked at the man and sighed. "Really? You and I both know it's a voice-changing app." She turned her attention back to Detective Taylor. "While he was busy grabbing the ten-thousand-dollar ransom from Murphy's Bike Shop," Carol continued, "I hid an iPhone beneath his car. We used a GPS app to track him here."

Detective Taylor did his best to hide his smile. "You can never underestimate the resourcefulness of a twelve-year-old."

"Look," said the man, "you've got this all wrong, if you'll just let me explain."

"I'm listening," said Detective Taylor.

"I do… uhm… *special deliveries* for people who require anonymity, if you catch my drift? You know, no questions asked."

Detective Taylor raised his eyebrows, as if saying, *Is that it?*

"So," the man continued, "I was told by a man to pick up a package from Murphy's Bike Shop. He said he would call me later with more instructions."

"So, you never met this man?" asked Detective Taylor.

"No, sir, we only talked on the phone."

"So, this mystery guy tells you to go get a package, and you go and get this package without any idea what it contains?"

"Yes, sir. As I said, I respect my client's anonymity. Look, the guy told me he would give me twenty-five hundred dollars if I agreed to do the job. I don't know about you, but twenty-five hundred dollars is a lot of cash."

"That's interesting," said Ava matter-of-factly. "You said that you value your client's anonymity, but I've got video of you looking in the satchel and counting the money."

The man glared angrily at Ava. She could tell that he was trying to figure out if she was bluffing or telling the truth. "I was just checking to make sure it wasn't a bomb. It's a dangerous world we live in—you can never be too careful."

Detective Taylor shook his head. "You've got an answer for everything, don't you, Mr....?"

"Smith...," he sneered. "Joe Smith. And if you officers don't have a search warrant, I'm gonna kindly have to ask you to leave."

Detective Taylor looked at Carol with a *please tell me you have more proof* look. "You said you had more evidence?"

"I do," nodded Carol.

"Wonderful." He turned his attention back to Mr. Smith. "And as far as you're concerned, we are investigating grand theft, burglary, and now an alleged ransom. So, I'm going to let Carol show me her evidence, and *I'll* make a decision whether we bring you in for further questioning or whether I can get back to my prime rib dinner." He turned to Carol, "Okay, show me what you've got."

Carol already had her tablet ready. She swiped her finger across the screen, pulling up the first picture from the crime scene.

"This plaster cast is of a footprint, right outside Mr. Hardy's gate." Using her thumb and pointing finger, she enlarged the image, zooming in on the footprint. "Officer Holland," said Carol, pointing, "would you please bring us Mr. Smith's boot?"

"Certainly," he smiled. Officer Holland retrieved the boot and brought it over to Carol.

"Thank you," said Carol. Detective Taylor took the boot from Carol, turning it over to reveal the sole. He compared the sole of the boot to the image on Carol's tablet. It was an exact match of the cast she had taken at Mr. Hardy's house.

"That print puts Mr. Smith at the scene of the crime," said Carol. "And before you ask, yes, I have the plaster cast of the footprint so your lab can perform a comparison analysis if necessary."

"A boot?" asked Mr. Smith incredulously. "That's all you got is a shoeprint? There are millions of boots like mine."

"Don't worry," smiled Ava, "that's just the tip of the iceberg. You know… you were quite sloppy."

Mr. Smith's face grew pale. "What do you mean?"

"Well besides the satchel filled with Mr. Hardy's money, I was also able to film inside your trunk," said Ava.

"What? How the heck…?" The man shook his head.

"Anyways," continued Ava, ignoring his outburst, "as you'll remember, a crowbar was most likely used to break into the kitchen door of Mr. Hardy's home—I present to you, exhibit A."

Ava held her phone so Detective Taylor could see the screen.

"The crowbar," smiled Detective Taylor, nodding.

"Yep," replied Ava. "I know it's not the best video work, but if I zoom in, you can see blue markings on the bottom of the crowbar. I'm pretty positive," she said, turning to Mr. Smith, "that when the crime lab tests the blue paint chips we collected against the blue paint remnants on the crowbar... they're gonna find a perfect match."

"Don't forget to add...," said Carol as she studied the sole of the boot. "I bet these blue paint flecks on the sole of the boot and this dirt will be matches to the paint and soil from Mr. Hardy's house."

Mr. Smith's face grew dark, his mouth tightening. It was as if impending doom had him in a stranglehold.

"And if this isn't enough, Detective Taylor," smiled Carol. "We also have a hair sample from the chandelier in Mr. Binxley's room."

She swiped to a picture on her tablet. "This image shows a hair from Mr. Hardy, and this is a hair that we're pretty sure is from Mr. Smith."

Detective Taylor smiled at the girls. "That's more than enough to bring him in for questioning and to hold him while our forensic team run their tests. The game's over," said Detective Taylor.

"Officer Holland, please cuff Mr. Smith and read him his rights."

Officer Holland helped the man to his feet, his head hung to his chest as he was handcuffed. The metallic click of the cuffs: so loud, so final. Officer Holland patted the man down, checking for weapons. He removed the man's keys and then reached into the man's back pocket, pulling out his wallet. He flipped it open to his driver's license. "His real name is Eric Wright—he's from Ashford, Connecticut."

Detective Taylor stepped forward, staring directly into the man's eyes. "Eric, you've gotten yourself into a lot of trouble. In the state of Massachusetts, grand theft carries a prison sentence of up to five years and a twenty-five-thousand-dollar fine."

Carol noticed Eric's knees buckle slightly....

"But," he added, "I'll talk with the district attorney and tell her that you cooperated. But we're going to need the dog, and some answers about who set you up to do this. So, I want you to think *really* hard, and I'm only going to ask you once. Where is the dog?"

Eric was quiet for a moment, as if considering one more final act of defiance. He cursed under his breath, surrendering. "He's in the basement... in the laundry room."

"Is there anyone else inside the house?" asked Detective Taylor.

"No, sir," Eric shook his head. "It's just me."

"Okay," nodded Detective Taylor. He grabbed Eric by the elbow and led him to his car. "Watch your head," he cautioned as he opened the rear door and helped Eric inside. "All right," he said, shutting the door. "I'll stay here with Mr. Wright. Officer Holland, if you would, please retrieve Mr. Hardy's dog."

"Yes, sir." Officer Holland jogged up the steps and disappeared inside the house.

Ava literally jumped up and down—she couldn't wait to tell Mr. Hardy that Mr. Binxley was safe. "I'm so glad this one is over," sighed Ava. "That man really loves his dog."

"You girls did an amazing job," smiled Detective Taylor. "You solved the case in record—"

"Sir," Detective Taylor's radio squawked. "The dog… the dog is gone."

11
MR. BINXLEY VANISHES

"Gone? How could the dog be gone? Maybe he got loose?" asked Detective Taylor.

"Checking, sir," Officer Holland's voice crackled over the radio, "but there's no sign of him."

"We'll help him look," said Carol as they ran toward the house.

"I'll take upstairs," yelled Ava. Carol gave her a thumbs-up as they rushed through the doorway inside.

"Sir," squawked Detective Taylor's radio, "this house belongs to a Joel Aveno."

Detective Taylor angrily flung open the door to his squad car. "Eric!" he growled. "Where's the dog?"

"What do you mean? He's in the house, in the basement!"

"No, he's not."

Eric's eyes opened wide. "He is, I swear! When I left to go get the money, I locked him in the laundry room with food and water." His mouth fell open. "Unless.... Oh great... he set me up. He took him," said Eric, shaking his head.

"Who took him?" demanded Detective Taylor, seething.

"The man… the man who hired me to steal Mr. Binxley."

"I thought you just dealt with anonymous packages," said Detective Taylor.

"Recently I've been trying to expand my brand."

A vein pulsed in the center of Detective Taylor's forehead. "Who hired you?"

"I don't know. Everything was anonymous, I swear. The man that hired me paid me twenty-five hundred dollars to steal the dog. Once I delivered the dog to him, he would pay me another twenty-five hundred."

"So, he was going to meet you and give you the money?"

"No."

"How was the exchange going to take place?"

"There is a wireless video camera in the laundry room. You know, so the guy could watch what was happening. He told me to put Mr. Binxley in the laundry room and leave him there. I wanted the money. I wasn't about to fool the guy."

"Of course not," laughed Detective Taylor, "you're an upstanding citizen. So, when the mysterious man verified that you had the dog, he was going to pay you another twenty-five hundred?"

Eric nodded.

"How?"

"He was going to put the money in the mailbox and send me a text—"

"When you say the mailbox, you mean at this house, right?"

"Yes, he was going to text me once he left the money. I was supposed to take the money and skedaddle out of town. Once I'd left the house, he was going to get the dog."

"And he knew you weren't trying to double-cross him, because he had a live camera feed watching the dog."

"Exactly," replied Eric.

"But making five thousand dollars from the mystery man wasn't enough for you, was it?"

"What do you mean?"

"You decided to make a little extra money by calling Mr. Hardy and demanding a ten-thousand-dollar ransom."

"Yeah... there's that. I figured, why make five thousand when you can make fifteen thousand? I mean, have you seen Mr. Hardy's house? Have you seen his loafers? It's not like he's hurting for money."

Detective Taylor shook his head. "So, let me be sure I have the story straight. You stole Mr. Binxley and put him in the laundry room. The man who hired you monitored everything via a wireless camera. Then, you had the bright idea to earn a little more cash and called Mr. Hardy to demand ten thousand dollars."

"Yeah," Eric nodded. "In hindsight, none of these were great decisions."

"Definitely not your finest moment. So, after you drove to Murphy's Bike Shop, grabbed the ransom money, and returned home, you discovered Mr. Binxley was gone."

"Well, I discovered that he was missing the same time as you. The worst thing is, now I'm out of twenty-five-hundred dollars."

"Yep," nodded Detective Taylor. "You could have used it for a good lawyer… you'll need one." He stood up and shut the door, as Ava, Carol, and Officer Holland walked down the steps with grim faces. Mr. Binxley had vanished, without a trace.

Ava looked at Carol, crushed. "What are we going to tell Mr. Hardy?"

"Nothing yet," replied Carol. "We're going to figure this out."

12
THE SECRET CAMERA

Detective Taylor gave the girls permission to ask Eric a few questions before they left for the police station.

Carol quickly fired off a series of questions while Ava recorded the answers with her phone.

"Have you ever met the man who hired you?"

"No, I already told the detective man that."

"How did the man contact you?"

"Let's just say he asked around… and the next thing I know, he's texting me. He said I came highly recommended," said Eric smugly.

"I'm sure," said Carol, playing into his vanity. "You were one of our hardest cases," she lied. "So, how did this mystery man get the money to you, if you never met him?"

"He texted me the address to this house. He said the family was on vacation and wouldn't be home for a week. Nice digs, by the way."

"I bet," smiled Carol to keep him talking. "So, how did you get the money?"

"The front door was unlocked, and just like he said in the text, there was twenty-five hundred dollars in cash on the living room table."

"I see," said Carol. "So you texted him to let him know you had the dog?"

"Sort of.... Well yeah, I texted him, and I set up a wireless security camera that he could log into. It was basically live video to prove to him that I had the dog."

"Wait, wait, wait...," Carol paused. "Is the camera still set up?"

"Of course. I just got back to the house when you guys and the cavalry arrived."

"Is it connected to a computer? To your phone?"

"To a laptop in the kitchen. I bought a piece-of-junk laptop from—"

Ava and Carol dashed across the yard into the house. They raced through the living room, into the kitchen. An open laptop sat on top of an L-shaped island.

Carol slid her finger across the laptop's touchpad. The screen jumped to life. "VAB Remote Video Surveillance software," whispered Carol.

The software displayed a live video feed of the laundry room. Another window displayed the visitors' IP addresses that logged in to watch the video.

"Dang," said Carol, disappointed. "No one is connected."

"Yeah, I didn't think our suspect would be hanging around viewing an empty laundry room."

"I know," agreed Carol. "It was worth a chance."

"Unless…," said Ava. "Maybe it saves a history of visitors. Like a browser stores cookies—"

"Already on it," smiled Carol. She looked up from the screen as Detective Taylor appeared in the kitchen.

"Any luck, girls?" he asked.

"We'll know in just a second," said Ava. "We're looking for IP addresses that logged in to see the video feed."

"You two scare me… you realize that?"

"We do?" smiled Ava. "Please continue…."

"Got it," interrupted Carol excitedly. "Look! There's only one IP address that visited the camera. The timestamp shows that the person logged into the camera this morning and then a little over an hour ago."

"That has to be our guy!" smiled Ava.

Carol highlighted and copied the IP address. "Now, with a little luck…." She opened the browser and pasted the address into a tracking website. Seconds later, a map popped up, with a red arrow directly over Main Street.

"Can you zoom in a little more?" asked Detective Taylor. The girls could hear the excitement in his voice.

"Yep." Carol moved the mouse over to a magnifying glass icon and clicked several times.

"That's the Concord Public Library," said Detective Taylor. "Our suspect has probably been using their computers."

"Can you imagine?" laughed Carol. "I mean, if you caught the bad guy at the library, I could actually say 'book 'em!'"

Detective Taylor shook his head. "I take back everything I said earlier," he smiled.

"Everything?" asked Ava.

"Everything."

13

CONCORD PUBLIC LIBRARY

Detective Taylor and the girls stood at the library circulation desk, waiting to be noticed. When it was apparent that wasn't going to happen during this century, Detective Taylor cleared his throat politely to make their arrival known.

The trio saw a brief flash of poofy white hair behind a computer monitor, followed by an exasperated sigh, and then the sound of a squeaky chair being rolled across the floor.

"Incredible!" gasped Ava.

A petite woman appeared behind the counter. A pair of horn-rimmed glasses precipitously balanced on the tip of her nose—an incredible feat. But it was her hair that astonished the girls. While the petite librarian stood less than five feet tall, her immaculately pruned, towering swirl of bluish-white hair made her over six feet tall.

It was the most incredible thing the girls had ever seen. Carol shook her head. She was quite sure this woman was singularly responsible for destroying the Earth's ozone layer, one can of hair spray at a time.

"Hello, Mrs. White," said Detective Taylor, breaking the silence. "I'm Detective Taylor, this is Ava, and this is Carol. I was wondering if we could ask you a few questions."

Ava watched as the woman inflated her cheeks like a blowfish, then slowly exhaled, as if she had suddenly sprung a slow, painful leak.

"Halitosis," whispered Ava into Carol's ear. "Toothbrush...."

Carol didn't respond; she was holding her breath. She fought the urge to touch her face, to make sure it wasn't melting from her skull.

As the woman slowly deflated, Detective Taylor used a maneuver he liked to call "the flash of brass." As if it were unintentional, he moved his arm back so the detective badge on his belt was in full majestic display.

He wasn't sure why, but for some reason, that symbol of authority had an incredible impact on people's behavior. It was like magic. He watched as her beady eyes glanced down at his badge, and there it was: The change in her demeanor was instantaneous.

"How may I be of assistance, Detective?" she asked, a hint of a smile at the corner of her lips.

"Mrs. White, we're investigating a serious crime—a dognapping. We believe that the thief was here this morning and used one of the library's computers."

"A dognapping," said the woman with a nasal voice, her face filling with disappointment.

Detective Taylor and the girls took a step back as Mrs. White began inflating her cheeks again. Ava bravely hid behind Carol. "I've got your back," whispered Ava.

"You got the police involved because your dog is missing?" She shook her head, waggling her finger at the girls. "These kids today, you'd call the police if someone stole your homework."

"You can do that?" asked Ava.

Detective Taylor shook his head and sighed, "No, Ava.... Mrs. White," he smiled, attempting to regain control of the conversation. "This isn't just an ordinary dog. This dog is a famous, world-class show dog worth over a quarter-million dollars." He waited a moment for that number to settle in. "You'll be helping us solve a felonious, grand larceny case."

"Oh...." He could see her wheels spinning. "I see." She looked at Ava sourly. "Why didn't you lead with *that* information? ... Today's youth," she continued, badgering the girls, "unable to separate the important facts from the minutia."

"I feel like I should be offended," said Ava, "but I have no idea what *minutia* means."

"Minutia means trivial, or unimportant," replied Carol.

"Now see," said the librarian, smiling and gesturing toward Carol, "there's a young woman who knows how to articulate herself. She'll go a long—"

"Thank you for the compliment, Mrs. White," interrupted Carol. "But time is of the essence, you understand?"

"Understood," said the woman, folding her hands on top of one another. "Please continue."

"We believe that the dognapper used one of your computers to monitor the delivery of the stolen dog. Is it okay if we take a quick look at them?" asked Carol.

"By all means. We only have two computers for adults. Most adults bring their own laptops."

"That makes sense. Thank you so much," smiled Carol.

"If you don't mind, why would he use our computers? They're outdated and slow as molasses," inquired Mrs. White.

"Most likely, he used a library computer so we couldn't track the IP address back to his personal computer," said Ava.

"Ah, very crafty," uttered Mrs. White.

"One might say, fiendishly clever," said Ava, eyeing the librarian.

"Sorry, I've already formed my opinion about you," declared the librarian, staring back at Ava. "Come," she put a hand on Carol's shoulder. "I've wasted enough of your time. The public computers are located in front of the children's media section." She pointed to a long, gray, marble-top table, with three cream-colored rolling chairs.

"Perfect," said Carol. "Thank you."

"You're welcome," smiled Mrs. White. "Happy to help." She leaned in toward Carol's ear—her breath nearly rendering Carol unconscious. "Please try to encourage your little friend to read more. Her inability to articulate is preposterous." Carol cringed as the old woman over pronounced the *p*'s in the word preposterous, spraying her face with old lady spittle. She could hear her dentures rattling around in her mouth.

"I'll do my best," croaked Carol, feeling her knees buckle.

"Perfect!" Mrs. White said breathily.

Carol felt something on her shoulder—she prayed that it wasn't Mrs. White's denture. Thankfully it was just her hand.

"I'll be at my desk if you need me." Carol smiled as the librarian and her tower of hair made their way back to the front desk.

14
HISTORY MAKES A COMEBACK

Carol slid into a cream-colored chair and tapped the space bar on the keyboard. The archaic screen flashed, then came to life. A small window appeared, prompting Carol to enter her library card number.

"You gotta be kidding me," Carol moaned. She looked at Detective Taylor. "Would you mind asking Mrs. White for a card number?"

"Be right back," he said as he gingerly approached the circulation desk.

"Why didn't you ask me if I had a library card?" Ava asked Carol. "I'm offended."

"Really? You're offended? Fine. Ava, do you have a library card?"

"No. You know I never go to the library."

Carol was about to strangle Ava when Detective Taylor reappeared. She turned and gave Ava the two-finger *I'm watching you* gesture.

"Okay," he said, smiling. "You have to turn away. She made me promise that I wouldn't divulge the secret default code. Also… she made me take a picture of her for the police report."

The girls sighed and turned their backs to Detective Taylor as he typed in the passcode to unlock the computer. He gave Mrs. "Eagle Eye" White a thumbs-up, confirming his success.

"Okay, Carol," he said kindly. "You're in."

Carol slid back into the seat and launched the Google Chrome. She typed *chrome://history/* in the browser. Instantly, a screen loaded with dates, times, and web pages visited. She began to quickly sift through the list of website addresses, looking for the wireless camera's IP address.

"It would have to be for this morning," suggested Detective Taylor.

Carol nodded, concentrating. "Nothing in this computer's history matches the camera's IP address, so we can rule out this computer."

She slid over to the next computer, waited for Detective Taylor to type in the password, and then loaded the search history by repeating the same search string as before.

"Great…," said Ava when the empty internet history page loaded on the second computer. "It's blank."

"Not blank," smiled Carol. "Someone has erased the history. Do you see the trashcan?" Ava and Detective Taylor nodded. "You can easily delete all the browsing history by clicking on the trashcan."

"So what do we do now if they've deleted everything?" inquired Detective Taylor.

"Not to worry, I still have a few tricks up my sleeve," smiled Carol. She looked up apologetically at Detective Taylor. "Do you think you could work some magic and have Mrs. White log me in as an administrator on this computer?"

"Now you're pushing it. I'll see what I can do," he winked.

Moments later, he appeared with Mrs. White. He was telling her that he would make sure that he included how invaluable her assistance had been in his police report.

"Yes, yes, a famous dog like Mr. Binxley is certain to make the news," he added.

Mrs. White waved Carol out of her seat. Then slowly, using her index finger, she tapped in the admin password.

"You're not going to install any destructive viruses on this computer, are you?" Mrs. White asked. "I'm responsible for the safety of our members."

"No, ma'am," answered Detective Taylor. "This is a serious police matter. I'll be monitoring Carol carefully."

This seemed to satisfy Mrs. White, as she relinquished her chair to Carol.

Carol's fingers flew across the keyboard. Detective Taylor smiled as folders popped open and hidden files appeared. A few more clicks and she was in the Google folder.

"Here's where the magic happens," she smiled.

A quick click and a window appeared, with a tab titled "Previous Versions." Suddenly a small window beneath the tab filled with previous versions of Google installs.

"In theory," Carol explained, "if I click on the version that says 'Today,' and click 'Restore,' it will reload the folder with all of the deleted files. And then for the grand finale, when I open Google...." Everyone waited breathlessly as Google loaded, "...you'll see...." She typed *chrome://history/* in the browser and waited as the page loaded, "...the history is back."

"You did it!" said Detective Taylor, excitedly patting her on the back.

"Big brain, you're amazing!" exclaimed Ava as she bounced up and down.

"Thank you," replied Carol, already scanning the list of web addresses. "There it is!" she yelled excitedly, jabbing at the screen.

At a desk nearby, a sour-faced Millennial guy in a man-bun gave Carol the stink-eye.

"Mind your business," tsked Mrs. White. "She's solving a historical crime."

"Impressive," whispered Ava to Carol. "The hair hath spoken."

"Bingo. He logged into the web camera at 10:33 this morning," Carol said. "Mrs. White...," Carol spun in her chair to face her, "...is there a way to find out who logged into the computer today? They have to enter their library card number, so there has to be some kind of record somewhere."

Mrs. White looked stumped. She tapped her index finger on her lower lip. "I'm not sure. Let me ask Tracy—she's the one who usually assists people with the computers."

"Thank you," smiled Carol, "that would be awesome."

"My pleasure," said Mrs. White as she scurried off to find Tracy.

"She could smuggle a giraffe through airport security in that hair," said Ava.

Carol snorted, imagining TSA frisking her hair. "The bad guy could actually be hiding in her hair, and she'd never know!"

"Detective Taylor," asked Ava. "Even if we find the person's name, do we have enough evidence to… I don't know… search his house for Mr. Binxley?"

"Not quite. We'll have enough evidence to question him, but as of yet, we don't have enough to search his property."

"Detective Taylor," a nasally voice called out, "this is Tracy, our computer expert."

The trio split apart like bowling pins. A bulldog of a woman, wearing an incredibly tight teal sweater and black leggings, maneuvered her way through the small group, commandeering Carol's chair.

"Louisa tells me you're looking for the names of the patrons who entered their library cards at this terminal?" asked Tracy. She turned and stared at the girls and snorted, and then whispered something to herself about the misuse of library resources.

"Yes, ma'am," replied Detective Taylor. "We're looking for people that accessed the computer between ten and noon today."

"I see someone gave you the administrative password," she said accusingly, arching an over-plucked eyebrow.

"Mrs. White typed in the password," Ava replied. "She didn't give it to us. And she did so under the watchful eye of a highly decorated career police professional," replied Ava, suddenly feeling protective of Mrs. White.

Tracy snorted rudely again—obviously they had stepped on her domain's toes. "It looks like three people accessed this computer within the time period you intimated: Robert Wang, Susan Lemont, and Douglas Morgan."

"Do any of those match the list Mr. Hardy emailed you?" Carol asked Ava excitedly.

"Already on it," said Ava, swiping her finger across her phone. "Yep!" she smiled and nodded. "Douglas Morgan, 157 Birchwood Avenue."

"Mrs. White," Detective Taylor said, "and Mrs...."

"Mrs. Adams," replied Tracy curtly.

"Yes, of course. Mrs. White, Mrs. Adams, thank you for your help and your expertise. As promised, I will write a glowing report about your help with the investigation."

Mrs. White's face beamed with pride. "And you'll of course include my picture, in case this makes it into the local news."

"Oh yes, of course," smiled Detective Taylor.

"Picture?" inquired Mrs. Adams, turning in her chair to face Detective Taylor.

"Ah yes," he said, fumbling for his phone. "She gets a picture, you get a picture... everyone gets a picture."

"One moment," said Mrs. Adams as she jumped up from the chair. Ava watched with fascination as Mrs. Adams pulled the hair tie from her ponytail and shook her head like a wild stallion. She sat back down at the computer, placed her hand on the mouse, then posed for Detective Taylor, raising her eyebrows coyly. "I'm ready," she whispered hoarsely.

"Dear God," muttered Carol under her breath.

Glorious, thought Ava as she watched transfixed by the peculiar behavior.

Detective Taylor shook his head, and then raised his phone. He was about to snap the picture when Tracy cried out. "Wait! I want to be standing. The lighting is much better this way." She stood, placed one arm on the back of her chair, leaned, and as rolling chairs sometimes do, it rolled from beneath her. She screamed as she crashed to the floor, flipping the chair on top of herself just as Detective Taylor snapped her picture.

"Whoa!" said Ava and Carol in unison.

"Got it!" called out Detective Taylor. "Go! Go! Go!" he shouted, motioning toward the front of the library.

"Thank you," called out Carol as Ava dragged her to the door.

15
THIS PHONE IS TRASHED!

Detective Taylor rapped his knuckles against the dark red door. Inside the house, the girls could hear a man's voice, shushing what sounded like a pack of dogs.

"Did you hear that?" whispered Ava.

"Yeah… but we can't jump to conclusions," whispered Carol. "Remember, this guy shows dogs too."

The door flung open, revealing a tall man dressed in black slacks and a black dress shirt with the top three buttons unbuttoned, revealing a Brillo Pad of black chest hair. He was holding a small white poodle with pink nail polish. The dog began yipping as soon as she noticed the trio on the front porch.

"Jezebel, quiet! We have guests." He stroked the dog's head a couple more times and then placed her on the floor. "Go find your siblings." The dog turned and gave the trio an indignant look, then pranced out of the room.

"Mr. Morgan?" inquired Detective Taylor.

"Yes…," replied the man, his eyes narrowing. He removed a pair of black, thick-framed glasses from his pocket.

"Holy moly, I think we made a mistake," whispered Ava. "This guy looks like Jeff Goldblum, the dude from *Jurassic Park*."

"Shhh," whispered Carol.

"Didn't I see you two on television this morning?" he asked, pointing a finger at the girls. His voice was silky smooth, perfectly calm.

"Perhaps," said Ava, "Did one of the girls have lustrous hair with perfect highlights?"

"Oh yes," he replied. "It was definitely you."

"We are *so* famous," Ava whispered to Carol out of the corner of her mouth.

"Mr. Morgan, I'm Detective Taylor. I apologize for our intrusion." He paused as a trash truck rumbled by, screeching to a halt at the end of the street.

Carol's eyes flew open wide. "Excuse me," she muttered while dashing off the porch. "Phone call." Ava looked at her bewilderedly, but Carol simply shooshed her away.

Detective Taylor looked at her, then turned his attention back to Mr. Morgan. "Seems she has an important phone call. Anyways, we're investigating the theft of a dog," he continued. He reached into a manila folder and handed a picture to Mr. Morgan. "Have you seen this dog?"

"Why of course. Everyone in the dog world knows this dog. It's Mr. Binxley. He's missing?"

asked Mr. Morgan, handing the photo back to Detective Taylor.

"Yes, he was taken this morning. Dognapped from Mr. Hardy's home."

"Oh my! Milton must be going insane right now. Such a beautiful dog…. But… I'm not really sure how I can help you, Detective."

"Well… that's the thing. I think that you may be able to."

"Oh, what do you mean, Detective?" asked Mr. Morgan suspiciously.

"We got a tip that led us to the Concord Library. Have you been to the Concord Library lately?"

"I go there all the time—why? It's a public library. I don't see how that has anything to do with me knowing anything about Milton's dog."

"Well, it seems that you used a computer today that accessed a web camera surveilling Mr. Hardy's dog. We tracked the IP address—"

"This is preposterous!" Mr. Morgan interrupted. "Are you suggesting that I had something to do with this? I reported my library card stolen yesterday. So whoever stole my card accessed that computer, not me."

"That's interesting," said Ava, watching a small, nervous twitch at the corner of Mr. Morgan's mouth.

"You see," said Detective Taylor, pulling a small bag marked "Evidence" from his jacket pocket. "This USB drive contains library footage from this morning, which you might find *very* interesting."

Detective Taylor held the evidence bag up to Mr. Morgan's face, making sure he got a good look. The blood drained from his face. "I was simply returning a book this morning."

Detective Taylor shook his head. "Oh really... which book?"

"My guess is *Crime and Punishment*," offered Ava.

"By Fydor Dostoevsky. It's about the protagonist's moral dilemmas," said Carol, suddenly reappearing.

"What the heck happened to you?" asked Ava. "It looks like you got into a wrestling match with a garbage truck—and lost."

"Well, that trash truck gave me an idea," smiled Carol.

"Carol," Ava sighed, "Does your therapist know you're dumpster diving again?"

"You went through my trash?" screamed Mr. Morgan. "Unbelievable. I want her arrested for trespassing."

"What's unbelievable is how much Lean Cuisine you eat," retorted Carol. "But... look what I found buried among dozens of boxes of his favorite meals.

"A phone," smiled Ava.

"That's right, and it has some amazing texts on it to a friend of ours—perhaps you know him? Eric Wright?"

"That's not my phone. I've never seen it before," he growled. "Someone must have thrown it in my trashcan."

"Easy," cautioned Detective Taylor.

"I thought you might say that, and that's what took me so long." She held up a small plastic baggy filled with tiny pieces of paper. "It's the receipt for the phone.

"So, the thief probably threw it away with the phone. There's an alley behind my house—people throw things in my garbage all the time."

"Interesting, because you see, the receipt has the last four digits of a credit card on it. I bet when the police pull your financials, they're going to find a match to that number."

"Tsk, tsk," said Ava shaking her head in mock disappointment. "You always pay cash for your burner phones, so embarrassing mistakes like this don't happen."

"Great job, Carol," smiled Detective Taylor. He turned to Mr. Morgan. "The game's up. We know that you took Mr. Binxley. I've already dispatched

Officer Graham from the Concord Police Department forensic unit. We'll be able to compare the fingerprints you so kindly gave me to the fingerprints on the phone, your texts, your phone calls—"

"I never gave you my fingerprints! What are you talking about?" interrupted Mr. Morgan hotly.

"Actually, you did. Remember the picture I handed you of Mr. Binxley? I didn't really need you to look at the picture. I simply wanted your fingerprints."

"You tricked me," he cried. "You can't do that!"

"Actually, he can," replied Ava, smiling. "Look, you got caught. You made some rookie mistakes. Try to do better next time."

"So," said Detective Taylor, "since I'm feeling generous, I'm going to give you one chance to come clean. If you do, I'll put in a good word with the district attorney's office for you." The detective paused, waiting for his words to settle in. "If not, you will be charged with grand larceny, possession of stolen goods, and whatever else the prosecution drums up. How does five years in the slammer sound to you?"

All of the fire disappeared from Mr. Morgan's eyes. He looked down at his hands as if to say, "What have I done?" He shook his head and looked up at the detective and the girls. "Twenty years," he said softly. "Twenty years I've been waiting to win a 'Best in Show' award. I traveled to Germany to buy the perfect dog. I spent thousands of dollars on Gretchen, a beautiful Cavalier King Charles Spaniel. Her eyes, her eyes...."

The girls watched as Mr. Morgan gazed toward the heavens.

"Oh, how they sparkle...."

"Is he going to be okay?" Ava whispered to Carol. Carol shrugged, caught up in the moment.

"And then Milton just traipses in with Mr. Binxley and wins the North American Best in Show award?! Stealing what was rightfully mine! *I* was supposed to win. *Gretchen* was supposed to win...."

Mr. Morgan began to sob. "I was supposed win, to be famous...," he whimpered.

"Mr. Morgan...," said Detective Taylor quietly.

"I know. I know." His head dropped in defeat. He stepped to the side, holding the door open for Detective Taylor.

"I never would have harmed him. He's safe inside... follow me."

16
HOME!

Detective Taylor screeched to a stop in front of Mr. Hardy's house. The girls sat in the back seat with Mr. Binxley, who was taking turns jumping from lap to lap and giving them slobbery wet kisses on their cheeks. They could see Mr. Hardy inside, watching television.

Detective Taylor looked over his shoulder at the girls and smiled. "Watching you two solve this case brought back a lot of memories of when I was a young detective. I had a lot of fun solving it with you. Thank you."

"We learned a *lot* from you," said Carol.

"Yeah," agreed Ava, "a lot." Mr. Binxley wagged his tail and barked.

"I think Mr. Binxley agrees too," laughed Carol.

"I thought the move with the USB stick was brilliant," said Ava. "You never said it was surveillance footage of him from the library; you simply said *some footage he would find interesting*."

"Criminals aren't the only ones who can be sneaky," he winked.

"We also had video on the laptop, from when he stole Mr. Binxley from Eric Wright," offered Carol. "I mean, if you need more evidence…."

"Would it be stole or re-stole?" asked Ava. "I mean, Eric stole Mr. Binxley, and then Mr. Morgan stole him again."

"Anyways…," said Carol, "I looked at the video. He wore a baseball cap and sunglasses, but you could still tell it was him."

"You girls managed to find a mountain of evidence… plus, he confessed. I'll put in a good word for him, but he'll have a long time to think about what he did," sighed Detective Taylor. "Speaking of a long time, Mr. Hardy's been waiting long enough. Let's get Mr. Binxley home."

Ava picked up Mr. Binxley from her lap and handed him to Carol. "You do the honors, Carebear. Without you, who knows if this case would have been solved."

Carol tried to object, but Detective Taylor insisted that Ava was right.

Carol scooped up Mr. Binxley into her arms. His eyes met hers and he licked her nose, making her laugh. "I can see why Mr. Hardy loves you so much," she smiled.

Detective Taylor walked around his car and leaned against the passenger-side door, watching the girls walk toward the house. Just as they reached the porch, Carol turned. "Aren't you coming?" she called out.

"No," he smiled, motioning her on. "You've got this one."

Carol mouthed *thank you* to him once more, then followed Ava up the steps onto the porch. Ava flicked a shrimp out of Carol's hair and then rang Mr. Hardy's doorbell. They could hear the sound of his footsteps as he ran across the living room and flung the door open. His hand flew to his mouth, as tears began pouring down his cheeks.

"My baby…," he cried. "My baby…."

Reaching into Carol's arms, he grabbed Mr. Binxley, who instantly became a wiggling, crying fur-ball of joy.

The girls, overjoyed, watched as Mr. Binxley licked Mr. Hardy's face and nestled into his arms, wiggling against his chest. It was a beautiful sight to behold.

Mr. Hardy grabbed Ava and Carol and pulled them in for a bear hug, thanking them over and over. The girls stayed for a few minutes with Mr. Hardy—who insisted on taking a dozen pictures of them with Mr. Binxley.

"Oh," said Ava, "before I forget…." She reached into her detective kit and removed two huge manila envelopes. "This is Mr. Binxley's paperwork, and this is your ransom money."

Mr. Hardy looked at them with astonishment. "You rescue Mr. Binxley, you catch the bad guys, and you get my ransom money back. Thank you, girls, so much," he said, shaking his head. "But I can't take that money."

"The money is *yours*," insisted Carol. "Detective Taylor cleared it. It's *your* money."

"No, I want you to have it. I insist on you keeping it." He put his hands on his hips defiantly.

Ava turned to Carol. "I may have an idea that we can all agree upon. How about we take the money and donate it to Best Friends Animal Society?"

"I love it!" said Carol. "They're a wonderful organization."

"Agreed!" squealed Mr. Hardy, literally bouncing up and down.

"Well, it's settled then," smiled Ava.

The girls gave Mr. Binxley another hug, and then hugged Mr. Hardy once again.

"We better get going," said Carol. "It's been a long day."

"Thank you so much for everything. You girls are welcome to stop by and see Mr. Binxley any time you want!"

"Thank you, Mr. Hardy," said Ava. "We'll make sure to do that. Bye, Mr. Binxley!"

Mr. Hardy grabbed Mr. Binxley's paw and waved goodbye to the girls.

As the door closed behind them, they could hear Mr. Hardy's animated voice, filled with joy.

"You know what? We did a good job today," said Carol as they walked down the sidewalk to Detective Taylor's car.

"Yes, we did," replied Ava. She glanced over at Carol, her face beaming with happiness. "What are you thinking about?" she asked.

"Mr. Binxley…," she smiled, "licking my nose."

Ava laughed and punched her shoulder. "He *was* cute."

"Yes, he was," smiled Carol.

"You know why he was licking you so much, don't you?"

"Because I rescued him, and I'm his hero?"

"Because you smell like Lean Cuisine," laughed Ava, plucking another shrimp from Carol's hair.

A NOTE FROM THOMAS LOCKHAVEN

Dognapped was originally written for the *Ava and Carol Detective Handbook*. The story was going to be used to teach many of the investigative elements used to solve cases such as fingerprinting, hair and fabric analysis, taking footprints, computer skills, etc. However, our editor thought that it might make a unique standalone where we see Ava and Carol solve a case using traditional investigative techniques.

I truly hope that you enjoy *Dognapped* and the slight detour from the other Ava and Carol stories. I absolutely love writing about their adventures, and I hope you enjoy reading them!

BEST FRIENDS ANIMAL SOCIETY

For over 30 years, Best Friends Animal Society has been running the nation's largest no-kill sanctuary for companion animals and building effective programs that reduce the number of animals entering shelters. To learn more about Best Friends Animal Society visit the link below.

bestfriends.org/about-best-friends

Thank you for reading *Dognapped*

Sign up for info on upcoming books at our website: avaandcarol.com

We hope you enjoyed reading the fourth book in the *Ava & Carol Detective Agency* series! Please leave a review on Amazon, Goodreads, or Barnes & Noble, we'd love to hear from you!

In *The Eye of God*, the fifth installment of the series, a famous Van Gogh painting has been stolen from the National Gallery of Art in Washington D.C. Or was it?

Turn the page for an excerpt from:
Ava & Carol Detective Agency
The Eye of God

1
NATIONAL GALLERY OF ART

The van lurched forward in a black plume of exhaust as it tore away from the curb.

Ava coughed loudly as the cloud of smoke engulfed her. Like a scene from *The Avengers*, she heroically emerged, shoeless, scraped up, but not beaten. A coy smile appeared on her face. *She may have my shoe, but I have her license plate...and her hair*, thought Ava, raising the old lady's wig to the sky like a trophy.

She paused mid-stride, before she forgot the license plate number, and texted *Virginia, LA1-568* to Carol. She then thanked the kind gentleman, who retrieved her shoe from the hood of his shiny red Mazda Miata, as she limped back toward the National Gallery of Art.

As she approached the gallery, she could hear the unmistakable voice of her mother.

"Ava Clarke, where did you...?" Her mom emerged. She noticed Ava's skinned-up knees and shoeless feet and cried out, "What happened to you?" She pulled her into her arms.

"I'll explain everything to you, Mom, but right now I think they want to talk to me," replied Ava, pointing to an avalanche of security guards and police officers spilling out of the doorway.

Thirty minutes earlier—Washington, D.C.

It was a typical muggy summer day in Washington, D.C. The only reprieve Ava got from the sunlight was her mom's shadow, which she tried to stay in as she and her best friend Carol traveled down a busy sidewalk to the corner of Pennsylvania Avenue and 10th Street.

"Stop!" shouted Ava, perhaps a little too loudly and dramatically—several pedestrians unglued their eyes from their phones and came to a stop.

"Not you guys," she clarified to the crowd. "I'm talking to my mom."

Ava ignored the angry looks and annoying comments from her mother because she was in the midst of what could only be described as a life-changing-encounter—and she just happened to be dying of thirst.

Wordlessly, she grabbed Carol by the arm and pointed with a shaky finger.

Carol's eyes grew wide. They had both experienced run-of-the-mill snow cone vendors in Livingston, Massachusetts, but here, on the sidewalk, stood the alpha and omega of all snow cone purveyors.

In unison, their mouths shaped the word: *Rainbowlicious*. Thirty-two, yes, thirty-two delectably delicious ounces of rainbow-flavored Icee. Ava's hands moved to her cheeks, bewildered. *How did they even know what a rainbow tasted like?* She shook her head; it was too much to comprehend!

"Mom, Carol and I are about to evaporate and die, but look...." She pointed at the Icee cart, decorated with a huge flashing rainbow and dazzling pieces of rainbow-colored ice falling into a massive cup with a swirly straw, guaranteeing *even more* deliciousness.

"Go ahead," laughed Ava's mom.

The girls scurried over to the vendor, afraid that it was too good to be true, fearing that, like an oasis, it would disappear at any second. Moments later, with gargantuan Icees in hand and disaster averted, the troop marshalled on to Constitution Avenue.

"Once we cross Constitution, we'll make our first stop," announced Ava's mom, pointing at a sprawling stone building. "The National Gallery of Art."

Carol's brain was literally salivating, without a bib. Yeah, she was a rebel. The night before, she not only immersed herself in the official National Gallery of Art website, but using her miniature notepad, courtesy of the J.W. Marriott, she plotted out all of the exhibits she wanted to see and her next optometrist appointment.

Ava too was immersed in deep thoughts of her own. She was desperate to find the nearest mirror, to see what her teeth and tongue looked like after consuming thirty-two ounces of rainbow-colored Icee. She stuck her tongue out as they walked, stretching it out as far as she could, trying to catch a glimpse of what she knew had to be amazing.

Carol's mouth fell open in awe; the building was massive. "Did you know that the gallery was modeled after the ancient Roman Pantheon, and the outside is made from pale pink marble from Tennessee?"

"That's fascinating," said Ava, turning her gaze skyward and staring up at the colossal columns that towered over massive wooden doors. "I'm more interested in those freakishly tall doors. They're like fifteen feet tall…basketball players must love this place!"

"Dude, the National Gallery of Art has over 141,000 paintings, drawings, photos, and sculptures! Pinch me! Please tell me I'm not dreaming!" exclaimed Carol excitedly.

"I think you need more than a pinch…perhaps counseling?"

The trio pushed through a massive door. A small cluster of people stood knotted in front of them, waiting to get through the security checkpoint. Two gallery guards dressed in white starched shirts and black pants manned each station.

One guard was assigned to search through backpacks and purses. Another waved a portable metal detector that looked like a miniature paddle over each person before they were allowed into the gallery.

"I wonder who created the sound that those security wands make," Ava mused. "Like in a testing lab somewhere, did a scientist say, 'This sound means bad, and this sound means good?'"

"Sounds have been used forever to mean different things," Carol said. "Haven't you ever watched *The Price is Right*? Bells mean something good, and buzzers always mean something bad. It's whatever we've grown to associate with those sounds."

"Thank you, Professor Miller," replied Ava sarcastically. "I was simply making an observation. But now I'll never be able to listen to a sound again without judging it…and you'll have to live with that."

A female security guard with thinly drawn eyebrows turned and scrutinized Mrs. Clarke and the girls. Her voice carried a certain edge of annoyance that must come, thought Carol, with years of repeating the same monotonous sentence over and over.

Eyebrow Guard continued, "Please place all electronic devices, cameras, keys, wallets, backpacks, fanny packs, and purses on the table. I'll be examining each item, and then Officer Weatherby will scan you with the security wand."

Ava watched curiously as a gentleman wearing a gray flat cap and carrying a collapsible easel and sketchpad chatted animatedly with Officer Weatherby, the security guard.

"Hello, girls. First time to the National Gallery of Art?" asked the large African American guard in a singsong voice.

"Yes, sir!" chorused the girls, smiling.

"Is he a famous artist?" inquired Ava, pointing to the gentleman ascending the stairs to the main level.

"Mr. Bumblewood?" asked the guard, turning his head. "Not that I know of. He's a regular, though. Been coming to the museum for the past few months. I've seen some of his drawings. He is very talented."

"It's really cool that you let artists bring their sketchpads and stuff."

"It's one of the best places to learn how to draw and paint," he said, smiling. "The works of art here have inspired many budding artists. Some of the most famous paintings and sculptures in the world are here. Monet, Renoir, Van Gogh…."

"I am so excited. This is a dream come true," said Carol earnestly. "I spent last night researching *everything* I could find out about the exhibits and the gallery online. Renoir is my hero," she cooed unabashedly.

Ava rolled her eyes—twice.

"Well, then, we need to get you going, don't we?" The guard waved the security paddle over them and smiled. "Clean as a whistle."

The girls thanked him and collected their belongings while he waved the paddle over Ava's mom.

"You've got two very well-spoken and polite daughters. You've done a great job." He smiled at her admiringly.

Ava blushed and just about gagged as her mom winked at the guard.

"They fooled you too, I see," said Mrs. Clarke.

Officer Weatherby laughed. "No, ma'am. I've got their number. I have three girls of my own, two boys, and eleven grandchildren…not much gets by me."

"I'm sure it doesn't," smiled Mrs. Clarke, and a mutual look of understanding flashed on both of their faces.

She thanked Officer Weatherby, collected her purse and phone, and then ushered the girls forward to a small clearing where they could talk.

"Okay, I have a meeting with Francine Morris. It should only take about an hour," said Ava's mom, unconsciously glancing at her watch.

"Not a worry—we'll be fine," assured Ava. "My esteemed colleague has already mapped out and color-coded the entire gallery by importance."

Carol nodded. "I'm a huge fan of efficiency."

"More like monotony," sighed Ava.

"Okay. Let's meet up in an hour. There's a huge fountain upstairs in the rotunda. It's located on the main floor," stated Ava's mom.

"Oh, I remember seeing that online," smiled Carol. "It has the Roman god Mercury on top of it!"

"The dude with little feathers on his feet and head? He's Mercury?"

"Yes," nodded Carol. "That's the one, as you so eloquently put it."

"All right, girls, I'm off," announced Ava's mom, giving them each a hug. "Carol Miller, she's your responsibility," she said, arching an eyebrow.

Carol smiled. "I've got this one, Mrs. Clarke. She'll be, shall we say, putty in my hands."

"Oh, I get it…because we're in an art gallery," Ava deadpanned. "Har, har, har. Art humor. So hilarious."

2
THE BELLHOP

Carol laced her arm through Ava's and began half-walking, half-pulling her toward the steps that led to the main gallery. "Come on," said Carol, waving her hand-drawn map, "we've only got an hour!"

Suddenly, Carol skidded to a stop at the foot of the stairs, her rubber soles making a *chirp, chirp* noise.

"What, you forget how to climb stairs?" asked Ava. "Lift one foot, place it on the step, then push off with the other one, then raise one foot, push—"

"Shhh," whispered Carol, placing her finger over Ava's lips and mushing them. "Do you realize what this is?"

"Yes, a violation of my personal space," said Ava, pulling Carol's finger away.

"This just happens to be a famous Pierre-Auguste Renoir painting! It's *The Young Soldier*," she whispered breathlessly.

"Are you sure?" asked Ava, squinting. "It looks like the bellhop at our hotel."

"It's a Renoir," gushed Carol. "Take a picture of me and the Renoir!"

Ava pulled out her phone and took several pictures of Carol posing with the painting.

"If you get any closer, he's gonna have to buy you dinner," laughed Ava.

Ava leaned in and read the tiny gold placard beneath the painting: "The Bellboy by Chaim Soutine 1945." Ava smiled. *I'll let her have her moment*, she thought.

"Okay, onward!" laughed Carol as she began to ascend the stairs. "This is amazing. We're here less than five minutes, and I've already seen a *Renoir* masterpiece."

"Earth-shattering," Ava called out as she struggled to keep up with Carol.

"Care-bear, while you revel in the moment," began Ava, stopping midway up the stairs, "can you give me two minutes? I need to run to the restroom. Thirty-two ounces of melted Icee equals a bathroom emergency. Plus, I've been dying to see if my teeth and tongue look like a rainbow!"

"Noooo! Two minutes would be an eternity to have to wait, and…," Carol looked at her watch, "…we've already burned through five minutes of our precious hour. Just meet me upstairs in the Van Gogh exhibit. It's in Galleries 91 and 92."

"What? I didn't hear you."

"Meet me upstairs in the Van Gogh exhibit!" shouted Carol emphatically.

"I didn't *ear* you. What did you say?"

Carol looked at Ava, annoyed. "There is one precious commodity I don't have a lot of, and that's time."

"Sorry. I was pretending like I didn't hear you. It was a little Van Gogh humor. Didn't he like chop off his own ear or something like that? I thought you would appreciate it."

Carol narrowed her eyes.

"And patience."

"What?!" asked Carol, whirling precariously on the marble steps.

"You said time was your only commodity, and I was just mentioning patience. You know, as another commodity."

Carol took a step toward Ava. "Five minutes. You've made me lose five precious minutes. I'll decide what your punishment will be later, but trust me, it will be tragic. Tragic, I say!" she called out as she marched up the stairs.

"Love you!" called up Ava.

"Tragic," replied Carol.

3
DON'T BLINK

Gallery 91 was a small, unimpressive gray rectangular room. The wooden floor was polished to a shine, and upon that floor stood a solitary bench where art enthusiasts could sit and immerse themselves in the works of great artists.

Gallery 91 connected to a slightly larger room, uniquely named Gallery 92. The slightly larger gallery, however, boasted two benches and connected to an even larger room, heroically named Gallery 93.

Ezekiel Martin was the guard in charge of these three rooms. He was a youthful seventy-four-year-old. He wore his salt-and-pepper hair short with a part exactly two inches above the top of his right ear. His crispy white starched shirt and perfectly pleated black pants represented his sense of pride and the seriousness he held for his position. Everything about Ezekiel spoke precision. Ezekiel had watched over this precious piece of gallery real estate for nearly twenty years.

Today, he was guarding six works of art by Van Gogh and numerous works by French artist Edgar Degas. Ezekiel exchanged pleasantries with a young bespectacled artist named Mr. Bumblewood, who thoughtfully made his way to Gallery 91 with his sketchpad and easel.

Today seemed like every other day, except unbeknownst to Ezekiel, Mr. Bumblewood had nefarious plans. He had spent months befriending the security guards, learning their routines and gaining their trust.

He had made sure that they had seen him countless times passing through the gallery, spending hour after hour drawing and refining his artistic abilities. He had gladly shown his latest work to the museum staff and had expressed his greatest dream of someday having his artwork hung in this auspicious gallery, beside the artists he revered.

Mr. Bumblewood had meticulously destroyed all suspicion and had fooled the very protectors of our nation's historical masterpieces. Inwardly, he smiled; he had lulled them into a false sense of security—and now, their mistake would soon make him rich.

Mr. Bumblewood didn't need to look up. He knew there was a security camera directly in front of him, festooned between rows of track lighting. He also knew that the camera wouldn't pose a problem—he had worked out every detail. He hummed quietly as he assembled his collapsible easel and placed his sketchpad on it.

To execute his plan, he needed to be alone in the room. Thirty uninterrupted seconds was all he needed, and this early in the morning, that shouldn't be a problem.

He knew that Ezekiel made his rounds like clockwork and that once he checked in on his gallery, he wouldn't return for another ninety seconds. Ezekiel's precision and strict adherence to routine would be his downfall!

Mr. Bumblewood looked up and smiled at the famous painting staring back at him. It was a self-portrait of Van Gogh. *Don't worry,* he thought. *I'm not going to hurt you.* He removed a fine-tipped charcoal pencil from his cloth carrying case. His heart beat a little more quickly than usual, and his breathing became slightly erratic. *Calm yourself. Calm yourself.*

He leaned forward and busied himself sketching, focusing, and breathing slowly through his silicone, prosthetic nose. His eyes subtly shifted to the side as a shadow draped across the floor. Mr. Bumblewood pretended not to notice. Inhaling slowly, he acted as if he was completely immersed in his drawing.

"Looking good, Matthew," said Ezekiel admiringly, using Mr. Bumblewood's first name.

"Thank you, Ezekiel," he said, looking up and smiling.

"Hopefully, someday, we'll have your portrait up on the wall," offered Ezekiel, pointing at Van Gogh's self-portrait.

"That would be a dream come true!" smiled Matthew broadly. "I'll have to sketch you as well," he joked. "I can see it now: *Historical Guardian of the National Gallery of Art!*"

"Shoot," shrugged Ezekiel, laughing. "After forty years of service, you'd think they would give me my own statue!"

"Seems like a given," agreed Matthew, nodding. "I'll put a letter of recommendation in the suggestion box for you!"

"Thank you, Matthew. I'll let you get back to it," said Ezekiel as he walked out the door.

Matthew waited a moment, listening as Ezekiel's footsteps grew further and further away. He reached down, swept his finger across his phone's screen, and typed *are we good?* Two seconds later, the word *yes* appeared.

Matthew placed the phone into his jacket pocket and then pulled out what appeared to be a second phone from the same pocket. Despite its appearance, this device was not a phone. It was a wireless jammer, and it had the ability to jam any video signal within fifty feet.

He pressed a button on the device. Five seconds later, the lone video camera in Gallery 91 suddenly went offline. He was now invisible to anyone monitoring that camera.

Matthew quickly walked over to the doorway between Galleries 91 and 92 and listened intently.

All was silent. Rushing over to his sketchpad, he flipped to the last page, which was completely gray. A piece of non-permanent, adhesive paper had been meticulously pre-cut and laser printed to be the exact same shade of gray as the wall behind the famous Van Gogh painting.

Glancing behind him once more, Matthew delicately placed the gray adhesive paper over the painting. Gently using a sponge, he smoothed out the wrinkles. He stepped back; the illusion was perfect. The gray paper in the frame made it look like the Van Gogh painting was gone!

He looked at his watch; he had forty seconds left before Ezekiel would make his rounds again. Matthew silently packed up his easel and sketchpad and quickly slipped through the doorway, nearly knocking Carol over as he raced down the stairs.

"Whoa!" shouted Carol, grasping the stair railing. "Art emergency?" she cried out.

For a brief second, they locked eyes, and then the man stormed down the stairs without uttering a word.

Okay, that was strange, thought Carol. She walked down a short hallway and paused in front of a gray placard that read: *Van Gogh Exhibit Galleries 91-92*. Excitement raced through Carol's veins—she'd been waiting her entire thirteen years to see this. She stopped at the doorway as a distinguished-looking guard caught her eye and smiled at her.

"Good morning, young lady. This is the Van Gogh and Edgar Degas exhibit. Currently, we have six Van Gogh masterpieces and twelve works by Degas."

"Wonderful!" exclaimed Carol. "Thank you so much!"

"Certainly," he replied, bowing slightly. "If you have any questions, just let me know. I've been watching over this section for over twenty years."

"Wow," said Carol, truly surprised. "I'm sure I'll have some questions for you. I'm betting everyone tells you they are here for Van Gogh's self-portrait."

"Ah, yes," he nodded. "It is one of our most famous pieces. It's actually the last self-portrait that he painted before his death."

"It's a shame that he died so young," replied Carol thoughtfully.

"Yes," said Ezekiel, nodding. "It's why I get excited when I see young people studying his work. Actually, a talented local artist, Mr. Bumblewood, is doing a sketch of the Van Gogh painting right now."

"Oh, cool," smiled Carol. "I'd love to see his drawing!"

"I'll introduce you," he said, motioning for Carol to follow him. As they walked toward Gallery 91,

Ezekiel noticed that Mr. Bumblewood's bench was empty.

"That's odd," said Ezekiel, hesitating. He scratched his head. "He was just here."

"Was he wearing a gray hat and carrying a sketchpad?" asked Carol.

"Yes. Yes, he was." Ezekiel looked at her quizzically. His pace quickened as he walked toward Gallery 91.

What's going on? wondered Carol.

As soon as he entered the gallery, his breath caught in his throat. The Van Gogh was gone! All that remained was an empty frame. Ezekiel leaned against the wall as the color drained from his face. His hand trembled as he punched at the radio on his shoulder.

"Code red," he spoke urgently. "Gallery 91, code red. Stop Bumblewood!"

Ezekiel turned; intensity filled his eyes. "What is your name?" he demanded.

Carol stepped back, shocked by Ezekiel's sudden attack. "My name's Carol. Carol Miller. Did-did that man just steal the Van Gogh painting?!" she stammered.

"Carol," said the guard, his voice filled with raw emotion, "you said you saw him leaving?"

"Yes, he nearly knocked me down the stairs. He was carrying a sketchpad and an easel. I fussed at him, and he just kept running."

Carol felt horrible for Ezekiel. His entire body was trembling. "Ezekiel, are you okay?" she asked, worried.

Ezekiel simply shook his head and sat down heavily on the bench, his hands grasping his knees. An alarm pulsed and strobe lights flashed. Within seconds the tiny room was filled with half a dozen security personnel.

~~o~o~o~~

Ava heard the alarm and scrambled out of the restroom. She raced to the stairs Carol had ascended just moments before, only to be met by a blockade of very serious-looking security officers.

"My friend is up there. What's going on?" she asked.

"There has been a security breach. You'll need to return to the main concourse. Wait there for further instructions," instructed a female guard.

"Security breach?!" Ava shook her head. *What kind of security breach?* she wondered. Ava grabbed her phone and texted her friend: *what's going on, are you okay?*

Ava & Carol Detective Agency: The Eye of God is available in all major retailers. Order *The Eye of God* today so you don't miss out!

If you love historical fiction, then you'll enjoy *Calista Chase Time Sleuth: Blackbeard's Treasure*. Great for ages 9-12 who enjoy reading time travel adventures.

If you're looking for a fantastical adventure filled with challenging puzzles, you may enjoy the much-loved series of *Quest Chasers*.

Learn about new book releases by following Thomas Lockhaven on Amazon and Goodreads, or visit our website at twistedkeypublishing.com.

Manufactured by Amazon.ca
Bolton, ON

30280912R00074